Lost American Fiction

Edited by
MATTHEW J. BRUCCOLI

The title for this series, Lost American Fiction, is not wholly satisfactory. A more accurate designation would be "Forgotten American Works of Fiction That Deserve a New Public"—which states the rationale for reprinting these titles. We are reprinting some works that are worth rereading because they are now social documents (*Dry Martini* and *The Cubical City*) or literary documents (*The Professors Like Vodka* and *Predestined*).

It isn't simple, for Southern Illinois University Press is a scholarly publisher; we have serious ambitions for the series. We expect that these titles will revive some books and authors from undeserved obscurity and plug some of the holes in American literary history. Of course, we hope to recover an ocasional lost masterpiece. *Weeds* was one. And this may be another. One of the volumes, *The Devil's Hand,* is truly a lost novel, for it remained unpublished for almost forty years. The Press is particularly proud of this discovery. It is our special ambition to resurrect more worthwhile buried novels.

At this point eight titles have been published in this series, with three more in production. The response has been encouraging. We are gratified that many readers share our conviction that one of the proper functions of a university press is to rescue good writing from oblivion.

M. J. B.

Robert M. Coates

YESTERDAY'S
BURDENS

With an Afterword
By Malcolm Cowley

SOUTHERN ILLINOIS UNIVERSITY PRESS
Carbondale and Edwardsville

Feffer & Simons, Inc.
London and Amsterdam

Library of Congress Cataloging in Publication Data

Coates, Robert Myron, 1897–1973.

   Yesterday's burdens.
   (Lost American fiction)
   Reprint of the ed. published by Macaulay Co.; with new after-
word by Malcolm Cowley, and with a textual note by M. J. Bruccoli.
   I.   Title.
PZ3.C6319Ye6 [PS3505.01336]   813'.5'2   74-23583
ISBN 0-8093-0717-0

CONTENTS

To

JIM THURBER

—*Who helped a lot.*

TOPIC SENTENCES, I.

The Days Go By In Strict Procession

"The Days Go By In Strict Procession . . ."

My present occupation is that of a book reviewer,
but I live in the country. Every day at half past one
the mail man arrives, bringing me the New York
Evening Post of the date of the day before. I carry
it to a chair on the porch, or to the lawn swing beneath the maple tree, and there, with deep interest,
I read yesterday's news.

It does not matter at all to me that the dance hall
bandit whose capture, wounded, after chase is reported on page three may, even now as I read, be
dead; that the crisis noted as looming between Russ'
—Japs, U.S. intervention seen, may have been ami-
cably averted through diplomatic action or have already reached its denouement in war; that the Schmel-
ing—Baer go is now over: the crowds dispersed, the
carpenters busy dismantling the ringside seats at the
Yankee Stadium, the two fighters home again, eating,
resting, answering long distance telephone calls.

Time ticks on at the same rate here as in the city,

but here I am nearer the axis of the pendulum and the moments pass with less violent a swing: the immediacy of the event is less important here. Troops may be mobilizing in Manchuria; Greta Garbo may have married or Mussolini been assassinated; the Sunset Limited may have split a switch near Sioux Falls, Ia., twenty killed, forty-three injured; this horse or that may have won at Pimlico. Like those persons who have traveled from east to west around the world, I am always one day younger than my fellows. I shall not know what is happening today until tomorrow. By that time, I shall be prepared.

But again there are days when the newspaper seems with silent inexorableness to point the futility of my position. The watcher idly scans the seas with his telescope; suddenly he perceives—how fatally far from his aid, yet seemingly how close at hand!—the struggling swimmer. He stares horror-struck, seeing with dreadful clarity every detail of the drama: the salt-soused hair, the thrashing arms, the agonized face puffed out with terror and tumbling with the waves, the gulping mouth uttering its inaudible cries. On such days I watch the world from my remote post, powerless to intervene.

10

I, turning the corner, passing the jewelry store, glancing casually down the dark alley, exchanging a cheering word with the discouraged merchant in his little notion store—I, by the mere accident of my presence, might have prevented what suicides, rapes, hold-ups, murders! Once, last winter on one of my visits to the city, I was taking an after-midnight stroll on Fourteenth Street: I was accosted by a beggar. Rather than fumble in my trousers, I gave him the handiest coin I had in the change pocket of my overcoat. He held it up in the light of a street-lamp: it was a quarter.

He tossed the coin in the air, caught it with a smack in his palm as it fell, he was obviously delighted. "That fixes me up!" he exclaimed, then turned and started walking rapidly toward Third Avenue.

I was going that way too. "What's your hurry?" I called after him. "I'll walk along with you." He let me join him; we paced along together.

"I was sure glad to see that two-bit piece," he explained. "Late like it is, too. I was just thinkin' I'd be left carryin' the banner tonight like I was last night."

He expressed no particular gratitude to me; he

11

hailed an impersonal good fortune. We passed the old Star Theatre, where a film celebrating the life of Al Capone was advertised. He denounced the man.

"Well, he's plenty rich," I remarked.

"That's a fact," said he, non-committally. For a moment, I entertained a wild idea of posing as a criminal myself, feeling him out cautiously at first, then openly propositioning him to join me in some desperate undertaking, with rich rewards in prospect. After his smug condemnation of Capone, the situation seemed to demand it.

Instead, we walked soberly onward, past the Central Savings Bank where a single electric light glowed in the dim interior; past Lüchow's, its flat black windows hiding untold quantities of sausages, sauerbraten, potato pancakes, marinierte herrings; past a policeman standing in a pose of heroic negligence, swinging his night-stick; past a drug store, a sporting goods store, a Photomaton, a clothing store, a shooting gallery. All night last night he had wandered, cold, hungry, unprotesting, among such phenomena as these; he had contemplated, apparently with no emotion but resignation, doing the same thing tonight.

He was a tall man, lean, friendly, sententious. He told me he came from Denver. I told him I had lived there, too. But he wasn't a native, he said. He'd been born in Pittsburgh. He'd gone west for his health. We spoke of casual things, both deliberately trying to give the episode the flavor of a meeting of chance acquaintances. We spoke as one business man to another. At the corner of Third Avenue we parted, he turning south toward the Bowery rooming houses, and I northward.

But I came home to my hotel and went to bed with a feeling of comfortableness at my heart: I felt that this once, definitely, unmistakably, I had been made the instrument of a kindly fate. What would he have done if I hadn't encountered him, if my hand hadn't touched that convenient quarter?

What are my friends doing, even now? Often, as I read my newspaper, I speculate as to their part in the day's doings. Were any among those who (names not given) suffered slight cuts and bruises as El train rams work car; were attended by ambulance surgeons and sent home? Were any present, either as onlookers or participants, at Police-Communist clash in Union Square? I am sure Henderson was there. Or was he that modest hero who, after snatching tot from path of mail truck on Eighth Avenue, vanished with a deprecatory gesture before spectators could obtain his name?

Was he passing and did he stop to join the watching crowd that jammed sidewalks and stopped traffic in Times Square as window-cleaner hangs from 19-floor window ledge, dropping to death as firemen mount ladder to rescue him? I am sure he was one of the guests, invited or not, at the Simon & Schuster tea for Will Durant.

I picture him chatting laughing with his lovely companion as he stands, bare-headed on the sidewalk, smoking a cigarette between the acts at the opening of Noel Coward's new comedy. His is the more valid existence, I tell myself: he deals with life on its own terms. He never looks behind effects to inquire their causes—he would as soon hesitate at entering a ball-room, to ask his hostess if the polished and resonant floor be staunch enough to support the dancers.

Undoubtedly, speakeasy proprietors unlatch their doors hastily and open them, bowing, when they see him standing in the vestibule. "Bon jour, Monsieur 'Enderson!" they cry, or "Buon' giorno, signor!"

He replies, with excellent diction, in either French or Italian as the case may require, and moves through the restaurant toward the bar, glancing languidly about him; he mingles familiarly in the fights at Tony's, after the theatre.

Afternoons, he is to be seen in the apartments of the more recherché commercial artists; of writers who are either just going to, or just returning from, Hollywood; of stockbrokers who collect, with a tempered enthusiasm, lalique glass and finance, every second year or so, an unsuccessful musical comedy. He is poised, alert, insouciant: he goes well with modernique furniture. I have not seen him for years. Nights, between the coming of darkness and the moonrise, I look southward down the length of my valley: cupped between the last hills and overflowing sluggishly into the sky I see a ruddy glow like a sullen aurora.

That is New York. I stare, wondering on what animated faces, what fevered gestures, on what scenes of kindliness or cruelty, of passion, joy or wrath that light shines.

15

"Here, as perhaps I've written you before, life is endlessly banal, endlessly satisfying." Here, there is no chronology. The hours are mere variants of light and shade, days lose their separateness, and weeks, months, years are embedded in the soft sure progress of the seasons.

Loveliest of all are these pearly days of early summer, or what is June—is it the pregnancy of spring that stirs then, or the impulse of summer already alive?

Tumultuously, Nature asserts herself, and man is dizzied by her tender exuberance. "You lie down in the open fields. You poke your fingers in among the grass roots and study the soil with microscopic eye. You stare at the sky as if it had newly come there: it is then that you are struck by the magnificence of clouds. Beneath you, the hills and the valleys stream out like a banner in the wind. Everywhere, is revelation."

Everywhere, one hears the heartening clack of hammers battling the wood, and the hypocrite whine of saws. One sees the carpenter, cheery and industrious, mitering his rafters, sheathing his walls.

The new house rises, the smooth new lumber glabrous and glittering as a fresh-peeled egg.

The days go by in strict procession. Wheat fields and oat fields show a scurf of green overlaying the rolled yellow earth: corn strikes up its spikes like the dragon's teeth. "Between us, this morning, we shot eight woodchuck—one a good hundred yards away.

"There was another, a female, which stayed stubbornly at the mouth of her hole, completely ignoring me as I walked up on her. Her young must have been out somewhere in the fields, for she was uttering frantic squeaks of warning. Have you ever considered—and has it disconcerted you—how much of that mother-love we prize so highly in our own kind is being expended all around us, unnoticed, by the other species?

"The bitch growling over its litter; the swallow darting from its nest and beating its wings in the face of the intruder; the woodchuck facing death on its threshold that a younger generation of woodchucks may live—in their actions one perceives a ruthlessness toward death that transcends instinct, that has a value as imperious and pure as the quality of life itself.

"I shot her, of course. They have a curious jerky

17

gurgling cry they give, as the blood bubbles into their lungs and they die. This was the first I had ever shot so close. There was something piteous about the episode—but then, they are such grievous things in a garden.

"Moreover, I could not but feel that as she choked and kicked and struggled—and even as blind death engulfed her—she knew that she had won her point. There were two or three infant woodchucks left hidden somewhere round about, to breed and breed again that their children's children might pester my children's garden. Who was it who said that all our wars are fought for our grandchildren?"

Dandelion have their golden hour and then turn ghostly; daisies follow them, dimpling the fields. In the garden, the beets, the radishes are ripe enough for eating, the beans go climbing hand over hand up their poles. Now, Procyon winks once in the first instant of darkness, then sinks down the western horizon, and the long tail of Hydra follows him; Venus grows dim. "Now, astronomically, summer is ended.

"Henceforward, the days will go slipping farther and farther down the decline toward the darkness of winter. Think of it! Summer is ended, and summer not yet begun. But is not all our life a series of such farewells?" Trout-fishermen whip their streams for the last time.

The nights grow more intimate, more caressing. The morning sun—its gentle, soft-born, measureless light—has a radiance like that of dreams: the world becomes dreamlike and our dreams our world; neither waking nor sleeping has either end or beginning. "The irises are out, and the sweet syringa. One can walk the fields and find wild strawberries everywhere.

"How can we hold in check these days that slip by so carelessly?" Pansies flutter like butterflies at the garden's edge. Furtively, among the dark leaves, the peony's bud unfolds. Passing the woodlands, one finds one's self suddenly swimming in the locust tree's incredible perfume.

Mountain laurel festoons the hillsides with grim beauty. "There is, of course, the great problem of whether or not I belong here.

"On all sides one sees writers, painters, fashion designers buying acres of tillable land or pasture and dedicating them to the cultivation of sumac, goldenrod and blackberry brambles. Is it for revenge? The artist's tendencies, it would seem, are always atavistic: he would raze cities, he would remake New England into a wilderness. But what of the land itself?

"I sometimes feel a strange uneasiness: the trees look hostile, the very grass seems to regard me with a venomous air. I have bought these fields and doomed them to sterility. Can you tell me if there is anything in common law concerning the rights of the soil to expect careful husbandry on the part of its owner?

"Wives, I understand, may in many countries obtain divorce if their masters fail in the discharge of similar duties." The days go by in strict procession.

Thunderstorms pass, aiming their lightnings with random vehemence. Under the downpour, the fields are drenched, quenched; a moment after, they are alight, alive again. "Evenings, we take an indescribable pleasure, watching the fireflies dancing over the brook. So hushed an activity, intricately tracing skeleton waves in the darkness—it is like watching the phantom of an ocean disporting itself."

Suddenly leaping, summer is upon us. In the first galvanic shock of heat, life takes on a reckless impetuousness: one must make the most of these halcyon days. The windows of the general store are gay with firecrackers, sheafs of roman candles, catherine wheels. Motor cars go hurrying on the highways; the very air is filled with an infinite busyness.

Nights, the moths gather like ghosts on the window screens or go fluttering flusteredly around the lamps; bats whip silently through the dusky air. The owl is heard, breathing stertorously in the tree. Days, there are the thirring of locusts, the buzz of bees, the hum of flies. Wasps spatter and drone along the attic window panes; crickets creak with absent-minded diligence. Hornets come roaming on angry errands of their own, lady-bugs wander humbly, blue-bottles blunder boozily in the sun. There is no silence anywhere.

Rise in the earliest hour of morning, lean from your window when the only light on the land is the flash of stars: by day, by night, there are a million murmurings in the ear of the loneliest listener, and the thin incessant singing creates in the hearer a sense of communion with all life. "Who would dislodge the milk snake from his cool retreat beneath the cellar door, or the black snake that watches, sharp-eyed and attentive, from under a stone at the water's edge while we go swimming in the pool?

"Who would harm the turtle, dragging himself with prehistoric clumsiness across the dusty road, or destroy the spider, that orang-outang of insects, as he swings his hairy body along the web? Are they not all part of us, as we of them? If the toad is crushed on the garden path, does not a fragment of our selves die with it?" One discovers an affection even toward grasshoppers, and with a certain fellow feeling watches them leap like little jumping jacks from the grass one walks through.

Now trees grow heavy with foliage, and sigh as one passes underneath; dust hangs heavy in the listless air. "The heat comes pumping in. Summer is upon us. But what a vulgar season it is: even the landscape goes a little *nouveau riche!* How pompous now the maple, and with what studied nonchalance the willow leans. Even the fields parade their wealth self-consciously; all the flowers, of course, are showing off. I pick my vegetables more in a vengeful spirit than in any other. 'Nature!' I say. 'I'll show her!' "

Summer is upon us: the days go clanging by, and one's head spins with the violence of their passing.

"We make some shift at playing games—ring tennis and the like—but most of the time I spend at the pool, digging boulders out of the brook bottom and piling them on the dam.

"This is a fascinating occupation. The pool is just deep enough now—about four feet—so that one must work with head under water to get within arm's reach of the bottom. So I scrabble away at the sedge-grass and silt, lifting my head to breathe and then plunging in again to peer about like a diver through the dim brown-green of the water; tugging, scratching out the packed sand and pebbles to find a better finger-grip; finally—with a heave and a kind of archeozoic sucking sound as the boulder breaks loose from the ooze that surrounds it—lifting the monster, all wet and glistening, to the surface.

"Then I float for a while, or crawl out on the bank to lie like an alligator in the sun, before tackling another one. But the best thing about this type of work is that, in a way, it pays double. By just so much as, in digging out your rock, you have lowered the bottom of the pool, so correspondingly you raise its surface level by adding the rock to the dam.

"Thus you extend top and bottom at once—no

mean engineering feat. On such hot days as these, I
find it comforting to think that I can work as lazily
as I wish at the pool, since at every move I am really
doing the work of two men."

Summer is upon us. The sun grins wickedly through
the crevices in the curtained windows, the heat goes
prowling in the darkened room. An animal ardor
stirs us all. "Tell me why, in that suspended instant
after love-making—tell me why one feels exactly as a
turtle must feel when you lift him suddenly into the
air: when with neck stiff-stretched and straddling
legs out-spread he scrambles frantically for a foot-
hold in the emptiness that surrounds him?"

Summer is upon us: the sun sets redly, reluctantly,
leaving the air still quivering along its track; early
next morning, choleric and unrelenting, it leaps to
the attack again. The moon is another sun, large, yellow, beneficently warm. "Driving along country roads
on summer evenings—the smell of hay from the fields;
the lights of distant houses, pocketed in the darkness;
the grass along the roadway, every blade rising crisp
and bristling as if startled by the glare of our headlights—why is all this so memorable?

"And the filling station one passes on the highway,

turning homeward—the filling station sitting superbly unreal in its own brittle illumination, a car halted dustily beside the pump and an attendant bent in a Grecian attitude of woe as he drains the last drops into the tank from the hose—the filling station no different from any other filling station, but never to be forgotten?''

Pegasus, gallant and gleaming, goes galloping over our heads; the Dipper is filling again. Huckleberries, in graceful tribute to Maître Joseph Gay-Lussac, bear their luscious fruit. Blackberries are thick in the brambles; elderberries hang in delicate strings along their branches. Grocery stores range ten-pound sacks of sugar along their counters; in every kitchen the preserving kettle boils on the stove.

Slowly the summer spends itself; evenings, there is a slice of coolness in the air, no thicker than a knife-edge now, but widening. Suddenly, the clatter of the harvester cuts across the fields.

"One has a sense of waking up, bemused as from too long sleeping." The year takes up its march again. "Everything now is in a fever of activity. We whirl about like particles in boiling water—the

25

Browns visiting the Billings's, the Billings's the Josephsons, the Josephsons the Burkes; the Burkes visiting the Cowleys and the Cowleys the Blumes. Where will it all end; or rather, how did it begin?

"Hurry, I've come to believe, is not a reaching forward. It is a reaching backward: an effort to hold off the future by greedily crowding into the present more than it would normally contain.

"Could one not, for instance, hurry backward? Or, to put it another way, the chief value of money is, or should be, to decrease the importance of time: it is the principle indictment of our civilisation that the wealthy are the greatest gogetters of them all.

"Theoretically, to the millionaire past, present and future are interchangeable. His money buys him immunity to the demands of the moment; whether he travel to Gaylordsville by airplane or afoot he will not be ruined, and so with the rest of his activities. To us others, however, a wasted minute means bread out of our mouths: we are always neck and neck with time.

"For instance, I drove up from Niantic the other day, through Hadlyme, East Haddam (which has somehow a reminiscent ring in my mind—have I rela-

26

tives there? Was it there that I spent some summer's
vacation as a child?), to Higganum (what names they
have!) and up along the Connecticut River to Middle-
town and so home. And I thought: these lovely Connecticut towns, nestling so peacefully in a past that
was so complete, so perfect in itself—what is to become of them?

"I should have liked to stop at East Haddam, walk
about a little under its elms, inquire if there were any
Coates's living there—to drop back, so to speak, a
decade or two into the past. But I had a book review
that must be written and mailed by tomorrow evening. I hurried on. We reached New Milford a little
after dark." Fruits ripen in the orchards; grapes
grow blue, their cordial clusters lustrous among the
pale broad leaves of the arbor. Wells that have been
dry begin to fill again, from that mysterious tide that
flows along the earth's rock floor.

The days go by in strict procession. Like little heli-
copters, the maple seeds make their death-defying
descents to earth; thistle-down is dandled by the wind.
The dry corn rustles and scrapes in the breeze. To-
bacco barns along the road bristle like porcupines, as
the vents are opened for airing. Tent moths spread

their spidery blankets over the trees.

All along the valley, one hears gas engines choking and sputtering in the barn-yards; hay is being got into the lofts, corn into the silos.

Waves of sumac creep crimson across the meadows. 'At sunset on September thirtieth, the year 5692 of the Jewish era begins.' In the depths of the woods, one comes upon one tree—a locust perhaps, or a sugar maple—standing all golden with autumn while the others have not yet begun to turn.

"But here, wherever one looks, there are pictures. Framed by the gilded branches of two regal maples, one gets a glimpse of a grassy swale, its slopes tumbled in innumerable tiny hillocks and peopled with clumps of miniature evergreens, among which trails the silver thread of a rivulet: it is unmistakably one of those secret little glades one sees in the background of a Titian or a Giorgione. There is an upland meadow that has the gray gleam of a Courbet; and the woods, the streams, are almost as prolific of Corots as the man himself was.

"Cézanne supervised the disposition of the fields and fences on the slope across the way, so that their

28

pattern might—oh, so subtly—supplement the slow curve of the ridge rising toward Stilson Hill. One comes upon woodland clearings where the leaves are as transparent and the air as laden with light as in one of those rare landscapes of Renoir. My outhouse doorway (seen from within, of course) frames in winter a Breughel, in summer a Pisarro.

"These, however, are the cream of my collection; now particularly, in autumn, one is startled to observe with what fidelity Nature reflects the worst aspects of the lesser painters—perhaps in gratitude because they strove so hard, on their part, to be true to her. Now every copse glows with the jellied browns of a George Inness, and the foliage is dyed and feathered like that in a Thomas Cole.

"All along the state road one comes upon parties of motorists halted staring at some vari-colored patch of woods, and oh-ing and ah-ing like Sunday visitors at the Metropolitan, among the Constables. There are sunsets by Turner, hay-mows by Millais, and cows by Benjamin West."

A day comes when the early riser sees the grass powdered with rime, and the roofs papered white with it. It is the first frost. L'automne est morte, souviens t'en. The days go by in strict procession. In the garden, all but the Swiss chard and the broccoli plants are wilted. Pumpkins and squash lie flushed and cosy among the withered vines; cows, nibbling the last pasturage in the brown meadows, look over the fences hungrily at them.

Garden furniture is got in; screens are taken down and stored in the attic. "We pack away deck chairs, dismantle the lawn swing and snug it down in the barn. One has a sailor-like feeling, doing all this: the house must be made ship-shape, to ride out the coming storms." Sportsmen look to their guns—the hunter's moon, ruddier even than the harvest moon, is rising.

Nights, the stars take on a contagious twinkle; the Pleiades reappear. Crows begin barking, planing over the vacant fields. There are butternuts and hickory nuts to be gathered: one comes home with beggar lice on one's clothes. Careful housewives collect sprigs of bitter-sweet and straw flowers and Japanese lanterns, peel pope's money, to decorate their houses. Old-fashioned people put bunches of hydrangea blossoms on the mantelpiece, to grow slowly brown through the winter.

The days go by in strict procession. There is a sense of calm in the air; light and shadow lie in formal, premeditated patterns across the road; the setting sun bedizens the windows of distant houses. Again, one turns one's attention to the clouds, watching them roll and multiply, watching them rippling and rumpling in the north, watching them cover the whole sky with glittering mackerel scales.

"This is the moody season, when the rain calls one out for long, lonely walks over the streaming countryside. One pries into abandoned houses, seeking the answer to some unnamed mystery. One takes shelter in old barns, stares with an indefinable interest at the curdle of straw and manure on the dirt floor, and listens to the creaking of a loose board in the siding as to an oracle." Now that the veil of leaves has fallen away, the massive structure of Nature becomes more evident: one sees the mechanics of the interlocked hills, one may study the architecture of the trees.

Naked, the ghastly sycamore postures in its leprous skin; the elm waves a languid fan against the sky. Imprisoned in the depths of the forest, the slender

31

birch gazes out through its bars in aristocratic disdain. Rising above them all, like a victim at an auto da fe, the martyred chestnut rears its mighty trunk in agony. "It is a time when the simplest truths seem to hold an inexhaustible content.

"One has a tendency to pin one's faith to commonplaces. I would say to the Communist: 'Consider my dog. Technically, he is my slave, but has he not enslaved me? He nuzzles aside the book in my lap, and I must drop everything to pet him. Whatever my engagements, I must calculate them so as not to disturb his feeding schedule; because of him, I can hardly stay overnight on my trips to the city.

" 'It is my duty to provide for him, and it is he who sets me to this duty. No glance is so reproachful as that of a dog whose master has betrayed him.' I would say to the capitalist: 'Consider my dog. We have a partnership through which nothing is produced, but from which both he and I derive profit. Technically, it is I who directs the enterprise, but he can at will supersede me.

" 'For instance, let me sell him for a sum of money to a neighbor. If he desires, he disavows the transaction and returns to me—what course is there for me to follow save to refund the money and receive him into partnership again? He over-rides finance by merely ignoring it. Affection and loyalty form his currency: it is valid only where he bestows it and negotiable only at his discretion. Beware that others do not follow his example.'

"I would say to all strivers, strugglers and contenders, to all toilers, moilers, ponderers, wonderers, worriers, hurriers: 'Consider my dog. He looks neither to the past nor to the future, yet he mocks you every day.' "

The days go by in strict procession. The moon drifts through its tangle of clouds; the trees sing as harps. These are gusty, blustering, flustering nights, when it seems that anything might happen—may indeed *be* happening, while one lies listening in bed. Lamps are early lit; the large room simmers with their yellow light, the wind goes fluting over the chimney top. "We played piquet till past twelve o'clock."

A crust of ice scallops the rocks in the brook in the morning, and the ground is brittle underfoot.

Buzz saws have been screaming in the woodlots; now the logs are cut and corded, and piled high in the woodshed, a sturdy barrier against the cold. "There is this to be said in praise of the farmer: he always knows that he has his back to the wall.

"Never for an instant does he relax his vigilance. Too often, to us others, there comes a conviction that the tide of battle has turned in our favor: we have worsted Fate, we think, and we rush forward hoping to make the victory a rout—never noticing, until too late, that we have been drawn into an ambuscade and the next attack may come from the rear.

"Not so the farmer. He is not misled by momentarily favorable circumstances; there is nothing millennial in his philosophy. Others may sit down behind their piled dollars and feel secure, but the farmer is always testing his fortifications: he knows that any penny's worth may be the keystone of his fortunes. Milk is the only dividend a cow gives, but that, on occasion, may be priceless. Let me tell you an incident that occurred to an old couple living not far from here, across the line in New York state.

"One morning, two winters ago, they woke to find the snow had drifted during the night until their whole house was buried in it. It was early in the season, and they had little store of provisions set by, but

34

out in the barn there were two cows, needing milking. The old man set himself to dig his way out to the barn.

"But remember that the drift was deep, and the temperature while the storm lasted down near freezing. In tunneling through snow, then, one is faced with the same problem as the prisoner who would dig his way out of jail: a means must be found for disposing of the material displaced.

"So the old woman got the kitchen fire going as hot as she could make it. Then, while the old man dug away the snow, she scooped it up in stew pots and boilers, melted it over the stove, and poured it down the drain. The drain soon stopped up; they stored the rest—so much more compact, of course, when melted—in kettles around the kitchen. Eventually, the old man made a hole he could crawl through, to the barn.

"He milked the cows, which saved *them*, of course; in the end, as it turned out, it saved the old couple, too. Before the thaw came, they were living on milk, and milk alone. This happened not much more than an hour's run by motor from the villas of Westchester county.

"Or, to disregard finance and human affairs, let us put it another way: the farmer's sole concern is with that one element which is constant in all equations—time. He knows the value of the moment, not as a unit of experience, but as the eternal connective between the approaching instant and the last. What will not serve as fodder must be made into ensilage; leavings from his summer dinner fatten his hog against the coming winter; at the height of August he is already looking forward to planting-time, next spring.

"Small wonder, then, at his scorn for the city-dweller's daylight-saving; long ago, he adopted year-saving, and moved his timepiece ahead accordingly. I find it difficult to know, at any given moment, exactly in what month or year—this or the next—the farmers around me are really living.

"Even, indeed, what century: alone among his contemporaries, he has, and has always had, a time-conception that exceeds his own life's span. Have you ever, passing among the smooth New England meadows, come upon one patch of land too steep for tillage or for pasture, and so left unworked through all our history? Mark the rubble, the rocks thick-scattered over it: that is New England, as the farmer found it.

"No, the farmer is our one humanitarian today. He adds a boulder to the stone wall, and drives the glaciers back a little further into man's past. He ties his roof with foot-thick beams, and saves unnumbered hours of labor in the lives of future generations.

"All your tractors, all your schemes for splitting this poor moment into further fragments will not beat him. He alone is a part of eternity."

Pheasant and woodcock are still to be beaten out of the copses; rabbit run helter-skelter through the grass. "What is there quite to equal the packed intensity of that instant when the bird bursts suddenly from the grass, and the eye runs down the swinging gun barrel and the trigger is pulled and the bird—the shot overtaking him just as he leveled off for full flight—drops stonily to the ground?

"There is a kind of fullness of experience in it that defies definition. It is as if the bird's course—the rise, the flight, the fall—had described the outline of all tragedy." In the sparser woodlots, the thin tree trunks rise like black bars against the level yellow of the leaf-strewn earth. Occasionally, in the early mornings, one

37

may see deer drinking at the brook, or playing grave delicate games among the alders.

Now the first flurry of snow whips down the valley, and the dog runs out and barks at it in amazement. "We had *boeuf à la mode* that night, with home-made rice wine, very good, and we sat thinking how long we had lived together. The nights are marvellously clear."

Distant sounds come nearer on the icy air. One can hear the trains on the Harlem Division, nine miles away over the hills, come rumbling down to Pawling, whistle, and go rumbling on again. "These early light snows—have you noticed the startling way in which they reveal our past? Like that powder used by the Bertillon experts, the flakes, delicately dusted over the meadows, betray every footprint made in our wanderings during the past year. The path to the pump is a white ribbon, clearly marked. Similarly, you can trace, though less distinctly, the course we followed to reach the pool, or the vegetable garden; and I can even make out, very dimly, the record of my movements in the half dozen or so times I visited, for pruning or spraying, the young pear trees I set out on the hillside last spring.

"It gives one an odd sensation, I confess, thus to look once more upon the embalmed face of the past. Another snowfall, of course, and it will be buried forever."

The mill pond freezes over; the rushes, pitifully divorced from their roots, are left standing straight as pegs in the ice. An expression of austerity comes over the familiar face of the landscape: the world waits, with a spinsterish resignation, for the boisterous onslaught of winter.

The day comes sullenly, peers broodingly in at the window, and is gone.

Flower—Holly DECEMBER, 1932 Birthstone—Turquoise
  12th Mo.   31 Days

Date	Birthdays of Famous People	Sun Rise	Sun Set
18 S	Edgar MacDowell, composer, 1861	7:18	4:34
19 M	H. C. Frick, steel, 1849	7:19	4:35
20 T	Harvey Firestone, tires, 1868	7:20	4:35
21 W	Albert Payson Terhune, author, 1872	7:20	4:36
22 T	E. A. Robinson, poet, 1869	7:21	4:36
23 F	Joseph Smith, Mormon, 1805	7:21	4:37
24 S	Kit Carson, scout and pioneer, 1809	7:22	4:37
25 S	Sir Isaac Newton, scientist, 1642	7:22	4:38
26 M	Admiral George Dewey, 1837	7:22	4:38
27 T	Dr. Pasteur, Bio. Chemist, 1822	7:23	4:39
28 W	Woodrow Wilson, Pres., 1856	7:23	4:40
29 T	Andrew Johnson, Pres., 1808	7:22	4:41

How Fast Do You Travel When
You Stand Still?

The Earth revolves on its axis once in 24 hours.
Its circumference at the Equator is 26,896 miles,
therefore anyone standing still at the Equator is carried by the rotating motion of the Earth at a rate of
nearly seventeen miles a minute. Those of us who live
in the latitude of the United States are carried at a
rate of from 12½ to 14½ miles a minute.

This seems rapid, but it is very slow compared with
the speed that the Earth makes in its orbit around the
Sun. This speed amounts to 1,588,765 miles a day, or
nearly 1,100 miles a minute. This will give us an idea
of the rate at which everybody on this old globe of
ours is hurled along.

DR. MILES' LITTLE PILLS   DR. MILES' LAXATIVE TABLETS
TWO TIME-TESTED LAXATIVES
FOR THE WHOLE FAMILY

Slowly, painfully, the world recovers from its sick-
ness; it does not die. Orion returns from his journey
to the Antipodes, Cassiopeia remains, as always,
seated in her stately chair; Jupiter is the evening
star. Coal chuckles genially in the furnace. The days
go by in strict procession. "This is the time when one
can take his profit on what he has done.

"I drink my own mulled wine, and when I rise to
change a record on the phonograph I test the floor
I laid to see that it does not creak; I inspect the join-

ings of the door-casings I put in place, the smooth surface of the table I built. These are joys stolen from past centuries. Who nowadays can point to a tree he planted, or hang his immortality on a nail of his own driving?"

The new applejack is casked and put down in the cellars; the last of the cider is set aside for vinegar. Sur le Noël, morte saison: one reads Villon, rises to change the phonograph record. "But let me tell you about this book I'm trying to write, in between bouts of book-reviewing.

"It's a novel, or rather a novel about a novel, or perhaps one might better describe it as a long essay discussing a novel that I might possibly write, with fragments of the narrative inserted here and there, by way of illustration or example.

"Or—again one might say—the attempt is to make it as nearly as possible a true example of the roman vécu. Nothing in it that I myself have not seen, heard, felt—or seen or felt in some other so vividly as almost to make the experience my own.

"The plot, of course, is the difficulty. You know my idea about plots—pick a good lively one and then forget about it. In this case, though, I don't think that formula would work. I have this young man, Henderson, and the process would seem to be to take him to the city and there lose him, as thoroughly as possible. Or at least to reverse the usual method, and instead of seeking to individualize him and pin him down to a story, to generalize more and more about him—to let him become like the figures in a crowd, and the crowd dispersing.

"But isn't that, after all, the authentic thing—the thing that happens to all of us nowadays, and to all our friends?"

The snow now lays its chill embargo permanently on the world. Under it, full three feet deep, the earth is frozen hard, and everything—rocks, fenceposts, seed and seedlings, the infinite small life of the soil, the shaggy thick-muscled roots of trees—lies locked in that iron embrace. "But often I think that music is the only means of describing a landscape.

"Those two lines of hills, rising and falling, endlessly intertwined: they have a harmony like that of two violins in a concerto. Trees against the snow should be played, *grazioso*, on the piano; and the winter's dusk comes like the sound of the oboe over the land.

"Have you ever noticed how a distant mountain rings out like a trumpet, loud and glittering, on the icy air?" Motor cars pass with a whirr of chains; on less frequented roads the way is drifted over, and sleighs make their own paths through the fields. Farmers let their beards grow, and cut their beef from the hung quarter with a hatchet. Nights, a kettle is always left simmering on the stove, to thaw out the pump in the morning.

In the back room of the town garage, warm and oily smelling, an unending game of poker goes on: under the table, a gallon jug of apple to warm the players.

Skis whisper in the snow. "Have you ever known, or can you imagine, a sensation so pure or one so swelled full spherical with its own sufficient loveliness as when, topping a rise on a ski run cross-country, one pauses and surveys the wide white expanse of virgin snow that lies before him? Untouched, unmarked: here indeed are regions that have never been

43

visited before, and whose very air has never been troubled by the commotion of a voice.

"Launching one's self, at last, down that smooth slope of stillness—it is like bursting the ball of being. It is like re-birth."

The days go by in strict procession: suddenly; it all seems endless, intolerable. The drear-eyed Winter has out-stayed his time; Nature, beset by her innumerable affairs, has forgotten us.

"What are you up to, Mother Nature? We sit by the fire and the fire grows cold; the sun glares down angrily at us and gives no warmth. Have you forgotten us, Mother Nature?

"Have you forgotten us, Mother Nature? We are alone here. The sky is stolid and unseeing. The fields lie buried. The trees are as lonely as ourselves. What are you up to, Mother Nature?

"The world lies dead around us. Nothing stirs or is soft to the touch. There is nothing to hear, to see, to smell. What are you up to, Mother Nature? Have you forgotten us?"

Suddenly, comes the thaw.

Suddenly, with the south wind, the air swallows the snow. Suddenly, the hard earth dissolves, lies formless and quaking; gathers itself again; becomes the sweet, easy, warm, wet and well-soaked soil where we walk, we lie, we roll. "One goes about simply looking, smelling, feeling. It is magical, the senses are confounded: one can taste the air, feel the soft faint perfumes arising, smell the life around him." Bulls are bellowing, horses whinnying. Birds come visiting; every day has the coolness, the sunny leisureliness of a Sunday morning.

Grass starts, and buds make tiny crocketings along the tree branches. The first crocus peers above the loam. Cows go rambling out to pasture, and barns are swept clean, flushed and aired. And now the first furrow is turned, the first field harrowed, the first seeds sown.

The last bit of clinker is cleaned from the furnace. According to ritual, the out-house box is dragged away, dumped at the foot of the orchard, and put back empty in its place again. Year-before-last's Sears Roebuck catalogue is burned on the trash heap.

A year has passed.

Motive

Let us suppose a lady is seated at the piano, but her fingers do not touch the keys.

It is the hour when silence (timidly, its pale face) gently turning:

It is the hour when all tall things (wherever they are: factory chimneys, trees, town steeples, city towers) taking one last proud melancholy look:

It is the hour when day (departing: gliding unseen unseeing above the happy oblivious throngs. Like a somnambulist, silently the day) moves blindly toward the abyss of night:

It is the hour of (twilight on the world; the mists begin to fall and (twilight: dying the day that has been sad and long. The darkness deepens and (the shades of night fast falling: weary the heart now but sweet the song as (in the mellow eventide. Only the

firelight gleaming as, dimly) the twilight and sweetly:
dreams of dead days, of still-loved voices, passed
beyond recall. A lady is seated at the piano, remembering a song and the lips that sang it as, softly) the
brooding twilight: low to her heart softly singing, the
twilight) shadows softly come and go. Her dream is
of love; and weaving into her dream comes (sweetly)
love's old song. It is the hour of) twilight: her fingers
have fallen from the keys.

It is the hour of (tenderly, the falling leaves, the
flowers: fading, the autumn) twilight:

Twilight: its last sigh (gently) lost on evening's
breast; is there music (faintly? The far guitar: soft)
on the air? A lady is seated at the piano; and though
the room is far from New York (in some southern
clime, maybe, where still the summer's roses live un-
wilting in the plentiful warmth outside the window,
and) the air is imbued with that blue which at such
times in the city seems to bring down the sky itself as
if palpably among the buildings. At such times the
city's towers shake their heads with a golden clamor,
looking down at us from a heaven in which we share;

crowds move rejoicing in processional, and the traffic of the avenues goes modestly singing like a choir of angels.

At such times Henderson would be seen in Madison Square meditatively strolling, or pausing to stare up awestruck at the diamonded windows prematurely welcoming the night, but the lady seated at the piano in her lonely room looks out through the wide-opened window on a landscape unlit by any light and but faintly stained as yet by darkness. He never recognized the features of her face, seeing only the blur of her mouth, her eyes deep-shadowed, and the spectral whiteness of her arms; he saw (in the flick'ring shadows, dimly) the smooth sad sculpture of her throat.

It is the hour when (dusk falling: in the heart) the twilight bringing back old dreams; and she at the piano:

Her fingers have fallen from the keys, but the last lost chord of the (melody: the old sweet) song she has been playing still hovers (fatefully: like the sound of a great Amen) over the thunderous silence of the room:

Night is falling, and a lady is seated at the piano; the lights have not yet been turned on. She sits silently, motionless in the gathering darkness, as if in hiding there she would surprise the secret processes of her desires.

Her dress is gray and its collar lies wide at the neck, narrowing just to hide, but still to hint at, the soft parting of her breasts. The sleeves (their folds perpetuating her last melodious gesture) have dropped away from her arms. No one is near; no one will come to her on that night or on any other, but as if wantonly to beguile her loneliness she has garbed herself in a style to delectate a lover. The stuff of which her dress is made clings tenuously to her body: so soft that it follows the smooth firmness of her thighs with voluptuous fidelity, so thin that her nipples appear as twin bubbles under its surface, so tightly fashioned that its texture would be as pliant and unwrinkling as the flesh itself to the head that would be pillowed on the tender hill of her belly.

Once, walking down Fifth Avenue on a windy autumn afternoon, he (almost, thought he) recognized her: she was descending from a limousine at the curb.

Her fur wrap, expensively trailing; she emerged from the cushioned interior: to the harsh pavement her unaccustomed toe. A footman held the car door. A buttoned doorman stood by to assist. Her slim shoulders never quite shrugging off their weight of Russian sable, her eyes remotely shining, her lips softened by a faint (oh! faint, and regally impersonal) preoccupied smile, she crossed the sidewalk and entered the portals of The Tailored Woman.

Henderson walked on down the Avenue, permitting himself to speculate in humorous husbandlike fashion on the purchases she would make in the shop.

Twilight: a lady is seated at the piano. Her fingers no longer touch the keys but one slender foot, extended, depresses the pedal which leaves the strings still vibrant with the last strong chord.

Her slipper is of dull black leather (something on the order of Spanish kid, or suède) and its sides are cut deep to display the high-arched instep.

Her stockings are of gray, as is her dress, but these are a darker, smokier hue, blue-tinged, and yet so gauzily woven that the mesh seems only thinly to veil the warm flesh within, and the swelling calf glows honey-colored through its misty shroud like a young moon not yet risen above the vapors of the lower atmosphere. Climbing yet higher, and (as when the soaring moon shines clear at last in the unclouded sky) her firm fair skin, out-distancing the stocking's reach, shows the more dazzlingly white for the dusky haze that shadowed it below.

The stocking-top is picot-edged, so that the embroidery runs in a row of tiny scallops along its border; and these (like lesser ripples on the ocean's swell) follow the hem as, encircling her leg, it strains upward to the garter-strap, sinks, and again rises, as do the enameled waves (motionless, yet endlessly advancing) that course the circumference of a Greek vase. Often, walking homeward late at night and seeing one high window still alight, Henderson would pause staring, wondering who it was that moved behind the curtains, and if she herself might not be there.

He was a young man, as I remember him in those early days, alone and lonely in the city: you would have seen him, long past midnight, walking in Times Square—in the yawning dawning the street a doomed emptiness and the rain voicelessly inquiring, and he wonderingly watching each belated passer-by.

You would have seen him loitering in the holiday
hustle of One Hundred and Twenty-fifth Street where
all day the crowds (and at night the lights, the windows) go whistling laughing, or one day when at
Union Square and (lost among the (men women:
hurrying, the) tall man the fat women, grayly (the
face as if crackling, and) the two and in shawls all
(hurrying) their feet freckling the sidewalk. It is like
a board walk: the Coney Island glitter of an
ORANGE PINEAPPLE DRINK stand and across
the street the open park-space (ocean-like) dilates the
air as, pausing by the news stand) you would have
seen him aimlessly wandering. You would have seen
him walking, and (always) walking to meet her: always (walking) in his mind a twilight sadness, and
the lady (dimly seen, and) seated at the piano.

It is the hour of (songs: faintly, at twilight) memories; a lady is seated at the piano.

Her torso, supple and erect, lifts itself effortlessly
and lightly, as if it imposed no weight on the cushioned haunches. Her fingers have fallen from the keys.

She wears no underslip, but her hips are enwreathed
by a lacy garment which, slashed high on either side,

encloses only the cleavage of her legs, cradling hammock-like the perfumed intimacies there. The lace of which the garment is made is dyed a smoky blue, to match the stockings' color; to it, at intervals along its border, are sewn small satin rosebuds, some purple, some pink, some white.

Her waist is sheathed by an elastic girdle, of the same rubber-threaded cloth as those bandages with which one sees a plaster figure of Venus decorated in some druggists' windows; from it, two tentacles reach down, taut, to either stocking's top, and this girdle, clinging as tightly to the hips as if it had grown there, clothes the middle of her body like a carapace, enhancing (as the turtle's shell its meat) the tenderness of the flesh within.

A lady is seated at the piano: in the (gloaming, the) twilight shadows softly come and go. Her head bends gracefully, listening and her shoulders leaning, but her fingers do not touch the keys. Her body blooms like a tall pale flower: only a narrow brassière (misty-blue, like the stockings, the lacy panties) encircles her bosom; through it, like eyes through the lenses of a pair of sun-spectacles, her breasts peer out with an air at once studious and shy.

It is the hour of twilight, and a lady is seated at the piano. Once, as he stood in a telephone booth downstairs in the Times Square Building, Henderson thought he heard her voice. He was calling the Buckingham Apartments to speak with a friend who lived there, and through some error at the central exchange he found himself listening for a moment to a conversation already in progress on another wire. ". . . but I'm not at all sure I can go with you, or even that I want to," he heard (thinly, distantly, but with a poignance of inflection that struck to his heart) an unknown lady's voice: "You see, I've always . . ."

The connection was abruptly broken. "Buckenam gdaftanoon," he heard the switchboard operator at his friend's apartments saying. He hung up, sickly, and with a feeling of helpless desperation as of one who has heard a summons and can not respond. Had it been she, and what had been the discussion he had surprised? To whom had she been speaking, and where had she been asked to go—to the theatre?—to a football game?—to some far haven in the Orient? Had the other been a suitor begging her to elope with him, and had she refused because she too was searching, in twilit longing, for an unknown lover?

It is (dimly, the fading) twilight: a lady is seated at the piano, her head bent low over the dying harmonies of the keys, and her body burns with an unattainable white beauty. Henderson never saw her face. He never met her, but throughout his whole life he would be (walking: you would see him skirting furtively the teeming sidewalks of Broadway at Ninety-sixth Street, where (the light from shopwindows rippling over faces passing: in the street the bus-tops looming like illuminated balloons, and all around him the tumult, the glitter, as) the crowds hurrying to Loew's Riverside, to Healy's Sunken Gardens, to Shubert's Riviera, to the Whelan's on the corner for a double-rich malted milk with whipped cream and an egg salad sandwich. You would have seen him walking up Lexington Avenue in the early evening, with light dripping drop by drop from the Chrysler Building and the lanterne of the New York Central tower coming up like a nocturnal sun over the houses, but always he would be) thinking of her.

Always (walking, and) with an absent-minded intimacy he would be fondling his memories of her, as one fingers a coatbutton come loose on its thread.

He was rather a romantic.

TOPIC SENTENCES, II.

Often It Seems I Have No Friends . . .

Often It Seems I Have No Friends . . .

My present occupation is that of a book reviewer, but I live in the country. Nights, between the coming of darkness and the moonrise (with dinner just finished, perhaps, and in the living room they are all seated around the table discussing, over the slowly cooling coffee, the British by-elections. "Why don't we all go down to Danbury to the movies some evening?" is said; "What we've got to do is be ruder to people we don't like," is said; "Well, next year I mean to get the water pipes under-ground. Then they can't freeze," is said. Making the customary excuse, I go out; I stand on the edge of the terrace and, submitting myself to the quizzical glance of the stars) I look southward down the length of my valley: cupped between the last hills and overflowing sluggishly into the sky I see a ruddy glow like a sullen aurora. That is New York.

I stare, wondering on what animated faces, what fevered gestures, on what scenes of kindliness or cruelty, of passion, joy, or wrath that light shines.

At regular intervals I go there, traveling by train and arriving at the Grand Central Terminal, usually after dark. I emerge on Forty-second Street, but instantly I am recognized as a stranger.

Taxicab drivers lean from their seats, opening their cab doors invitingly, urgently offering to take me to a good hotel. The lights whose quintessential glow I had watched from afar, seen now close at hand, seem to be as impersonal and as arbitrarily grouped as the stars that shine—but more distantly, and with a milder defiance gleaming—on nights in the country.

Emerging from the Grand Central Terminal, I must plunge in the midst of these dazzling constellations, striving as I go to recognize the various clusters, to differentiate between motor car headlights and street lamps, to disentangle the lettering of one electric sign from that of another. I must walk westward on Forty-second Street, neither too fast nor too slow, but at the pace the others set for me; if I do not, passers will stare, taxicab drivers will scrutinize me, newsboys will jeer, crowds will gather, a policeman will be called. Doubtless, I shall go to jail. My whole appearance will be against me.

Often, I have loitered in the Grand Central Terminal for upwards of an hour, studying the books in Womrath's windows, the shirts in J. P. Carey's, the toys in Mendel's—postponing the moment when I must emerge, plunge in, walk onward. Often, I have nowhere to go.

Often, it seems I have no friends—or rather, I have friends, but all of them have Watkins, Algonquin or Stuyvesant telephone numbers and live in the Village. Tonight, I will have none of them: I know so well what they are doing. I know so well those green-tinted apartments, the furniture that has so much the air of being fresh from the furniture store, the standing lamps arranged to illuminate the pages of the books no one ever has time to read in the easy chairs.

There will be greetings and ringings of the telephone, cocktails will be poured and drunk, cigarettes held in nervous fingers. Towards eight o'clock or later, women will be crowding before the mirror in the bathroom, men will be hunting out overcoats from the tangle of clothes on the bed in the alcove and shoving their arms into the sleeves; people will be going trailing laughter down the stairs. We shall all gather on the sidewalk in a little noisy cluster, deep down among

61

the silent unfriendly houses. We shall debate the merits of this restaurant or that.

Taxicabs will come angling in to the curb; dome lights will shine on the men's backs bent over the folding seats, on the women's silk legs, white faces, and will flash off again as the doors are closed. Cigarette ends, spitting sparks like lighted dynamite fuses, will be snapped from the cab windows: we shall sit in our warm dark cubicle, peering out at the multitude of lights flowing past us like the lights of an alien world, as the taxis go scudding up the avenues, weaving through the side streets, toward this restaurant or that.

There, the waiters will pull tables hastily together, clean table cloths will be unfurled over the wine-stained ones. There will be a mêlée of orders for antipasto, crab-flake cocktails, Martinis, minestrone. The head-waiter will be suave, smiling, patient, and faintly disdainful. He will say that there are no more crab-flake cocktails.

There will be a girl at another table—a girl in a gray dress, perhaps: a girl whose face is turned from me, but whose beauty I can see reflected, sun-like, in the rapt moon-face of the man seated opposite her.

She will be sitting there, enfolded in an intimate atmosphere of her own and gravely eating celery: a girl with the smooth supple hands of a musician and (the dark head leaning as if (at twilight? A lady is) seated at the piano, and) I shall be staring hopelessly, knowing that I shall never see her again.

After the biscuits Tortoni have all been eaten, we shall go back to someone's apartment and, parking our highball glasses on the mantel-piece, play ping-pong until a little after two. Yet, however late prolonged, the evening must end at last. Farewells will be called from the stairs; the host will close his door and turn disconsolately to face the empty room. The rest of us will taxi home together, dropping off one by one at our separate corners.

As each descends, he will be seen for a moment waving gallantly in the snowy light of the street lamp. Then, as the taxi starts off down the endless avenue, he will turn away and vanish; or rather, as he moves —as his body (like the living core of a statue, emerging) breaks forth from the attitude in which we left him—he will have ceased to exist as himself, as the friend we know and remember. He will have become (suddenly) another nocturnal figure slipping, furtive and anonymous, among the dark shops, the silent houses, and indistinguishable from any other that one might encounter on the empty street, hurrying no one knows whither.

Who has not at some moment recognized, with a start almost of dread, that the life of even his dearest friend is involved in mystery? A subway train draws in to a crowded platform. Facing you, as the door slides open, you perceive a friend issuing from the car you are about to enter. You direct a greeting to each other over the heads of the crowd and exchange places —he, mounting to the street you have just left; you, perhaps clutching the very strap his hand relinquished, continuing on uptown—your errands neatly dovetailing.

But what were those errands? Was it a look merely of surprise that crossed his face as he saw you? Or did it contain embarrassment and annoyance at thus being singled out, given a name, among the nameless numbers in the crowd?

You come upon another, walking with an air of purpose late at night on an unfrequented street. You accompany him to the end of the block, too amazed at finding him thus to dare ask his destination. At the corner, while an elevated train—rocking, rumbling, dragging a transitory illumination along the high faces of the buildings—passes overhead, you exchange a few unintelligible words.

Then, with a nod, he hurries away. You cannot follow him where he is going. Have you never, seated at lunch with a friend or of an evening in his apartment, seen his glance grow suddenly opaque, heard some inconsequent remark escape him, observed an unfamiliar gesture—and realized how much of his life must forever remain secret, even from you?

So it was with Henderson. I still recall my feeling of amazement when, on being introduced to a young lady at a party, I heard her remark that she felt as if she knew me already: Henderson had spoken of me so often to her.

"Oh! He's always talking about you!" she exclaimed. "About the way you live all alone up there in the country and so on. I feel as if I knew all about you already."

I was smiling and nodding, saying: "So you know Henderson? He's a swell fellow"—and she, with extravagant hilarity: "Do I know him! If you'd seen him last night at my place you'd say I did. Was that boy tight! But he's a lot of fun though"—but inwardly I was startled and bewildered. I knew so little about him.

When I had last seen him it had been a chance encounter down near the docks, and he had shaken my hand without much enthusiasm, gazed at me out of eyes defiant and blue: he'd been down at the pier seeing his wife off on the "Lancastria" for a trip abroad, he'd said. He was too busy to get away now himself, but he might join her at the end of summer; meantime, she'd be visiting friends in Paris, and maybe take a trip through the Low Countries.

I understood, too well, what that meant. Among the people I knew, in the period after the war, a wife went abroad alone for a year as an invariable prelude to divorce. The trip was a kind of indemnity the lady exacted of her husband, in lieu of alimony, for the failure of their marriage.

She would go to Paris; she would stay at a hotel near the Rond-Point or the Etoile, but frequent principally the Rotonde; she would meet Harold Stearns. She would enjoy a tremendous but transitory popularity because she didn't mind paying most of the bill at Zelli's or at Bricktop Smith's; she would be generous with champagne, only demanding the right to weep on the nearest man's shoulder, when the gayety of the scene, and its impermanence—and the sense that somehow, in spite of its dash and movement, something was lacking—became all at once too much for her.

Abruptly, she would want to go home. Half reluctantly, half hopefully, one of the men in the party would volunteer to accompany her. There would be smothered caresses, struggles, kisses in the taxicab, then a kind of feline acquiescence until the cab had arrived at the door of the man's hotel; then there would be bitter and outraged refusals. Obediently, the driver would head for the markets: she would have discovered that it was a soupe à l'oignon at the Chien Qui Fume she really wanted. The man would drink calvados, and beer; she, cautiously, coffee: by a process of saturation, she would dilute his passion.

Afterward, at the door of the taxicab that was to take her to her hotel alone, he would exert himself to address her farewells that would be bitingly ironic, searing but suave: he would be swaying slightly as he did so. Suddenly, by a receiving look, a melting gesture, he would be overwhelmed with desire again.

He would find himself in the car, and her in his arms, and the taxi tearing out the rue Saint-Honoré: she would be lying back, all ivory in the chill light of the flitting street lamps, while his fingers fumbled at hooks, tore at her shoulder straps, scooped at the soft flesh under her armpits, funneled over the secret softness of her breasts. Her breasts would come out; he would stare at them lying there innocent and calm in their nakedness, and suddenly he would be kissing them as if he would drown them, and sucking at the alert little nipples: she would be watching him, proudly, contentedly, motionless.

Her skirts would be yanked up, and thrust down again. Their legs would become entangled, the rough cloth of his trousers shoving between the silk-stockinged knees, burrowing between the clenched bare thighs. His hands would drive up toward deeper recesses still; her hands would repulse him, but her mouth would be open and draining kisses from his. The cab would stop at her hotel just in time.

Often, she would reach her room with her dress half ripped away, but always with her virtue still intact. Next morning, she would go on a tour of the antique

shops on the rue de Seine and the rue Mazarine, looking for longer and more fantastic ear-rings.

I felt sorry for Henderson, thinking of all this. I
knew, too, that in thus confronting him while the farewells were still bitter on his lips, the taste still salt in
his mouth of the sea she must sail across to be rid of
him—I knew that I had brutally intruded. Given time
to forget their last tormented night together—the
tears, the miserable expostulations, the kneelings one
before the other—he would have been able to arrange
his story better, to speak with more assurance, if not
more plausibly.

My very presence now (here, on the tattered carpet
of market refuse, among the stale smells, the greasy
walls of Washington Street: the whole scene dingy
and dim as a tenement hallway, and I with bold au-
thority confronting him. I had burst in on his
thoughts like a police officer raiding a room at midnight, and he stood blinking sullenly, barring the
doorway and the secrets within: I, questioning him)
seemed peremptory and insulting.

I managed to say something or other, and got away
as soon as I could, making an appointment for lunch

which I believe one or the other of us later called off. But I watched him, that summer; he went from bad to worse. Towards the autumn, I came upon him sitting on a bootblack's stand, at the corner of Fifty-third Street and Seventh Avenue—but indeed, this was but one of our encounters.

I have seen him facing me as the door of a subway car slid open at a crowded station: he emerging and I entering, perhaps to seize the very strap his hand had relinquished. I have glanced up and caught him staring down at me from the top of a Fifth Avenue bus. Looking up from my table in a speakeasy restaurant, I have seen him enter, glance languidly about him, and move toward the bar.

I have visited him, evenings at his apartment, parked my highball glass on the mantel-piece, played ping-pong. Late at night, I have met him walking with an air of purpose on an unfrequented street. I know that he lived for a time somewhere out in Westchester: his car, driven furiously, has often overtaken mine on the Sawmill River Road. He has waved to me, smiled briefly; then—motor humming high, tires oilily skirling, the rear deck of the roadster making a dancing glitter—his car has thinned away down the road before me.

Later, I heard that he had lost his job, and there were stories that he had been seen, ragged and woebegone, mooching along the Bowery. When I ran across him on that street, however, he was top-hatted, in evening dress, and slightly tipsy: he had left an extravagant but very dull party uptown, he said. Here, he said, the people were at least not poor in spirit.

I remember, too, that once at a drunken gathering he arose unexpectedly and delivered a most extraordinary harangue. He spoke rapidly and with that prophetic vividness which intoxicated men can sometimes command.

I can not recall precisely what he said, but it was to the effect that, obeying a sudden impulse on his way to work the previous morning, he had called out to the elevator boy, "Eleven," instead of "Six"—the number of the floor on which the firm that employed him had its offices—and that the resulting experiences had altered the whole course of his life. I have no doubt that his intention was allegorical.

It was soon after this that his wife departed for

Paris. There were conflicting stories about that. I know, however, that it was at about this time that he paid me a curious visit in the country.

I remember I had just been sorting out a batch of books for review that had arrived by the mid-day mail when I heard the prolonged rasping scream of a motor horn in my driveway. It was Henderson, seated at the wheel of a bright green roadster that I knew didn't belong to him, with a girl in a gray dress by his side.

His appearance thus was a total surprise to me, and I suppose I showed it; moreover, my uneventful life in the country had begotten in me a kind of crusty resentment of anything that upset my usual routine. Like a hermit emerging from his cave, I imagine, I opened the door and stared at them; and they, on their part, perhaps to mitigate my unwelcomingness, put on a greater show of hilarity than before.

"Hi! I thought we'd find you!" he called as I approached, while the girl, jumping quickly from her side of the car, cried, "I see what *I* want!" and with a swift cool smile for me ran lightly past me across the lawn to the outhouse.

Henderson was sitting sidewise in the car seat, his

long legs dangling through the opened door. "We won't stay long," he assured me, with an odd, half-mocking, half-appealing smile. "I know how busy you are."

But, now that my first surprise was over, I was glad to see him, and I assured him of it stoutly. "Non-sense!" I replied. "I'm not doing anything special. And besides, you know how often I've tried to get you up here. Come on in."

He eyed me a moment, still with that odd, veiled smile, and suddenly I knew that there was some pur-pose, as yet unavowed, in this apparently random visit. Then, slowly, he slid his feet down to touch the running board and stepped to the ground. "Well, we were just driving around," he said vaguely. "I thought we'd drop in."

"Fine!" I said. "But tell me, where'd you get the car? I thought you'd sold yours or something."

He was rummaging in the recesses of the folded roadster-top. "I did," he answered over his shoulder. "This is the girl friend's." Then he turned, with a bottle of whiskey in his hand. "Here," he said. "We brought this along for you."

"Swell!" I began, a little embarrassed. "But I've

got lots of apple around—," but just then the door of the outhouse slammed, and the girl appeared around its corner, walking demurely toward us.

She was, I noted, not so young as she had at first appeared—indeed, there was a beginning look of matronliness in the fullness of her figure—but she had a warmth about her, an easy rich-flowing vitality that was directly, even sexually, inviting. She kept her gaze fixed on Henderson as she approached, and smiled up at him while he performed the introduction. Then she turned to me, but even then her eyes did not meet mine: instead, she fastened them on my mouth, as if she were more interested in the movement of my lips than in the words they uttered. It is a trick that I always find at once confusing and provocative.

Her name, I learned, was Mrs. Sennitt; and she lived in Briarcliff; and yes, it wasn't far from where Henderson had used to live; and she admired my view and my vegetable garden; and no, they'd had no difficulty finding my road. But between each answer she turned to Henderson, as if for guidance and instruction, and this gave a curious effect of irrelevance to all my conversational efforts. I felt like an actor for whom no part had been written in the play, and whose remarks only interrupted the progress of a carefully rehearsed scene. I led the way into the big living room.

"Oh! But it's enormous!" she exclaimed politely.

"Yes, and he built it all himself," said Henderson.

"Did you really?" she asked, and we all sat down. So we talked, but even as we talked I had the feeling that our words were but a surface covering, and that something else was afoot. Henderson had risen and was moving restlessly about the room, inspecting the odds and ends on the mantel-piece, the big map of Paris on the wall, and wherever he went her eyes followed him, as if she waited for him to make the next decisive move. I felt, in a way, that she only spoke to me to remind him of her presence in the room.

Suddenly he turned. "Say!" he cried. "We haven't cracked that bottle yet. Where's glasses and things?"

"In the kitchen," I said, reaching for the bottle.

But he had already picked it up. "Well, come on then," he said, and led the way out of the room.

There had been a brisk purposefulness in his manner that made me suspect a manoeuvre, and I half imagined that, once we were alone together in the kitchen, he would have some confidences to impart. And perhaps that had been his intention, for he hovered about while I poured the drinks, and even followed me down cellar to fetch the ginger ale. But he said hardly a word the while, and I came back bearing my own and the lady's drinks as much mystified as ever.

She was still sitting, motionless, on the couch where we had left her, but she raised her head slowly as I handed her the glass.

"Thanks," she said, and now for the first time, unexpectedly, I found her deep deliberate gaze entering and absorbing mine. And I was as if lost therein. For her eyes had a quality of clear translucence, an unplumable brilliance as if, like the sky itself, their blue was the bright pure blue of depth alone, and not of any color. And the irises were so intricately flecked with light, and that light so constantly changing, that one felt almost irresistibly impelled to move closer, closer and even closer, until the whole field of vision would be filled with their unshadowed luster. For a moment I stood over her, frankly staring, and she gravely unfalteringly receiving my stare.

But indeed, from the moment the glass had touched her hand, I observed a subtle transformation in her manner. It was as if the very feel of it, like the feel of his sword-hilt to the fencer, had given her confidence. She made herself at home now in a way she had not done before, settling back comfortably among the cushions and talking blithely and unselfconsciously, while now it was Henderson's turn to watch her as if trying to estimate the meaning behind her words.

He gave her hardly time to finish her drink and then poured her another one, while I went down cellar again to get more ginger ale. When I returned, however, they had finished off their glasses straight, and were standing together in the middle of the room.

Henderson turned as I entered. "Listen," he said. "We've got to be getting back soon, but before we go I thought I'd like to take Laura for a walk and show her your brook and so on. D'you mind?"

"Why, of course not," I said. "Let's all go. Wait till I—"

His wink halted me. Swiftly but unmistakably, he had winked at me. "No, no," he took me up smoothly. "I know you've got a lot of work to do and we've kept you from it long enough. We'll just run along by ourselves and leave you to get some reading done. Come on, Laura."

Then I knew. Then I knew the whole of it, the reason for their pauses and their hesitancies and their secret inquiring glances each to each. And though I hoped I had not shown my surprise I saw, when I looked at her, that she knew I knew, and the mutual knowledge made a curious, almost brother-and-sisterly bond between us. Her eyes had a strange look of gallant humility ("You know what I am now, and so you must take me. I am what I am," her eyes seemed to say to me) as she turned to follow him out the door.

A moment later, from the window, I watched her running laughing—her stocky but well-shaped legs flying, a glint of white flesh showing as the skirt climbed unregarded above her knee—down the steep slope behind him.

Escape, I thought: we've escaped him now. Let's hurry. I thought you were going to keep me there all day listening to that stuffy talk of his, and we with so little time to spend together. So let's hurry. Help me through this fence or had we better go down to the gate or climb over it: anyway, let's hurry.

Let's leave him to his books and his room that he built himself. Let's hurry. Where shall we go—there

where those pine trees are: wouldn't they hide us?—
over in that long grass: wouldn't that be secret
enough? Anyway, let's hurry: take me somewhere,
anywhere, where I can feel your weight pressing down
on me, the hardness of your body entering mine and
my body receiving it. Where your face can make a
sky for me and your lips close out the air and your
arms fold a darkness around me. Over there where
those little trees are? Let's hurry.

I watched them disappear among the young alders
down by the brook bank, and when they came back
an hour or two hours later I knew how she had looked,
as if I and not Henderson had seen her.

I knew how her wide hips lengthened into the full
firm thighs and with what soft pressure they could
hold a lover; how warm the belly was and how ripely
swaying the ungirdled breasts. I knew, as if I had
tasted it, the milky flavor of her breath, and I knew
the honey that could be drawn from her lips. I knew,
and I knew she knew that I knew, and we sat silently,
she lying passively on the couch and I watching sullenly.

Henderson fidgeted, then glanced at his watch.
"Time for one last drink before we go?" he suggested.

"I suppose you'll soon want to be rid of us?" he added casually to me.

Suddenly, my patience was at an end. "Well, to tell the truth," I answered with a brusqueness that surprised myself. "I *have* got a lot of work to do."

Henderson stared; but she, who had been lying passively watching us on the couch—she rose and came indolently toward me across the room: she came to me and, slipping her fingers softly in my hair, pressed my head back gently so that again our eyes met, and in her eyes I saw an appeal and a musing understanding. "Say it ain't so," she demanded, lightly teasingly.

I smiled at her, and for the first time felt that our moods had met and been linked together, completely, indissolubly. "It ain't so," I repeated obediently. "Do stay."

Her hand lingered against my cheek as she turned away. "I wish I could," she said. "But there are certain reasons why I must be leaving. Come on, darling."

A few minutes later they were gone, the car flitting swiftly down the road and, at the curve at Evans's (beyond (I knew) the red barn the white house at

Rehack's impassively awaiting their coming: at the curve at Evans's) finally vanishing.

They never came back again.

Henderson: I am trying to tell you the story of his life, but I realize there is little enough that I know about him. A hand would be laid on my arm, arrestingly, one night as I stepped from the curb to cross the trickling glitter of Times Square: it would be Henderson, smiling with a contained amusement as I turned in surprise.

It would be Henderson, seen through a flutter of faces as the crowd swarmed out through the theatre lobby on a gala first night, or Henderson whom I encountered unexpectedly at the home of an acquaintance: he would be leaning against the wall by the radio cabinet, tinkling the ice in his empty highball glass, his expression stiff and abstracted.

"I didn't know you knew the Tishmans," I would say.

"I don't. Who the hell are they?"

"Why, they're the people that live here."

"Well, let's get out of here then. I don't like the name."

81

"But how'd you get here, though?"

"Oh, I came with a crowd. Thurber, the Sayres—whole bunch of people. They've gone some place else, I guess. Must have, by now. What do you say, shall we take the air?"

But now, having decided to go, abruptly he would decide to stay. "No, I tell you what. You go if you want to; I think I'll stick around for a while. There's a girl here I'm trying to make." He would give me a smile too wide to contain its cunning; I would perceive that he was pretty tight.

"Tell me where you'll be and I'll join you later," he would say, and such was the persuasiveness of his manner that, though I had been enjoying myself well enough at the party up to then, now that our plot was hatched I would leave at once, to wait for him at the speakeasy appointed—where, like as not, he would never appear.

Or, parting at Fifth and Fifty-second Street, with the sun a bright sweet sadness on the onrush of the avenue—parting hurriedly after having lunched together. "God! I've got to run!" he would cry, glancing at his watch, beckoning a cab, shaking my hand,

adjusting his hat—all, it seemed, in one swift movement. "I've got a date and I'm late for it now.

"Ring me up next time you're in town," he would
call to me as (the cab door closing, the cab itself drifting—slowly—out from the curb. I would see him
leaning forward on his seat to give a direction to the
driver. Then, and (the pitying sun with glint with
sparkle, striking cripplingly: the host of motors hurrying endlessly in the warm bright haze, and) his
cab lost piece by piece among the red black blue: the
green bus charging) he would be swept away (like:
suicidally) in the flood of traffic—I often wondered
whither.

He was handsome at that time, and prosperous; his
coat sat well on his shoulders; his trousers hung neatly
down his legs. Waiters always came at his call. Bar-
tenders instantly obeyed the summons of his eye. At
the time of which I write, he was thirty-five years old
and a little over, and he had precisely thirty-two years,
nine months, and fourteen days to live. Sometimes,
at night, he would lie sleepless, feeling the weight of
those days, months, years pressing down inexorably
upon him.

For Henderson was doomed to live, as he was

doomed to die. He had, in fact, died four times already.

He had died once. The first time he died was when he was still a lad in Rochester, attending West High School, and one Saturday morning he took the family car and, accompanied by a school mate named Harold Barbour, went for a day's outing at Lake Ontario.

They drove through Sea Breeze, its shacks and shabby hotels shut now since the winter; then out the Lake Road winding, rolling, skirting the shore. Near Forest Lawn they parked the car in a meadow by the lakeside and went for a walk along the beach.

The time was early spring, and none of the vacation colony had yet arrived. The sun had a thin vernal brightness; the sea washed softly up the sand, but from the shore—with its clutter of boat houses, beach pavilions, its shuttered summer cottages among the trees—came no sound. They were at that age of adolescence when melancholy is the simplest emotion, and they walked idly, skipping stones, saying little, beset by a sea-borne sense of sadness, as if all the world were lonely. Their way led them toward the

84

point of a spit of land, and it was there that death awaited them.

As they rounded the point, the sea and the shore on the other side of their jut of land came suddenly into view—the sea, the sky, the shore spreading and receding toward wider deeper distances until all three melted together and were lost in the haze and the sea-glitter.

Rounding a point of land by the seaside on such a day of spring—it is always as if one came upon a new world, still with the soft fresh twinkle of creation upon it. Henderson had an instant's vision of this: an instant—then, not ten paces away from him down the beach but half hidden behind a pile of rocks, he saw a man with a rifle, and the rifle aimed directly at him.

It was an instant, and it happened long ago, but Henderson could always remember it: the sea, the sky, the shore, all dim in the brilliant distance, and black against the scene the man, his head masked murderously by the gun sights, and the round venomous eye of the rifle barrel. The man stood there (rather, it was as if he hung there, imponderable but portentous as a cloud over the bright vista) an instant with rifle poised and Henderson remembered the surge of rage that flung him—sucked him, even—forward as the gun was fired (its report hardly heard except as a part of his own rage speaking: he in that instant dying) and a flirt of smoke flicking past him; and the man's face lifted white and staring, the man receiving his onslaught like that of a spectre, in unbelieving terror, and he snatching at the rifle barrel and shouting and his fists hammering.

It turned out that the man was a boy no older than himself; it turned out that the boy had been shooting not at him, but at bits of driftwood floating in the water; it turned out that, thinking the whole beach deserted, he had carelessly aimed so close along shore that Henderson, coming unexpectedly around the point, had moved directly into his line of fire. But Henderson had learned that death can rouse one to wrath so great that self itself is annihilated in it, and death is quite outdone.

He died twice. The second time he died was when he was a student in Naval Aviation, during the war. There had been that first early morning when, arriving fresh from ground school, he reported for flight training at the Commandant's office at Bay Shore;

86

and afterward he had slipped down toward the beach between the hangars and had seen a covey of planes passing close above the water, and suddenly they had begun cavorting in a series of little dips and bounces, hilarious and inexplicable, as if they performed some jolly graceful dance on the unbelievable resiliency of the air (three zooms, he later learned, were the signal to break formation, and one usually added a few more just for the fun of it) and it had seemed the most utterly lovely thing he had ever seen.

Then there had been the marching here and there to various classes in gunnery, radio, navigation (with always the throb of motors in the dome of the sky, and high overhead those wings glinting in the sun). There had been a day or two of sitting waiting in the shade beside the squadron hut on the beach—the shade hot from the sand-glow, and the air stinging with the smell of salt and grease and gasoline—while one by one his companions had their turn in the air.

Finally, a plane had come taxiing lumberingly in, as clumsy as an old barge, and had shoved the nose of its pontoon against the sand. Two gobs in waders switched its tail around, then carried its two occupants, instructor and student pilot, pick-a-back to the shore. A young officer came to the door of the hut and stood dangling a greasy helmet.

"Student named Henderson here?" he inquired lazily.

Henderson got to his feet, but with more the sensation that it had been the ground that dropped away, and not he that had risen.

"All right, Henderson," said the officer, looking him over. "My name's Weil, and you'll be under me for instruction. We'll give you a hop now."

He had been carried out to the plane and loaded into the rear cockpit. Then, the motor idling and the propellor clacking over slowly, they sat there for a time while Ensign Weil, a spare brown man with an absent-minded scowl and an air of dawdling confidence, ran briefly over his instructions. "You know all about the controls, I suppose," he said with faint irony. "Yours and mine are hooked together, so when I move anything here in the front cockpit, yours'll move too.

"That's the rudder bar I'm kicking now. See it? Works like a Flexible Flyer. The stick's there between your legs. Push it and you go down. Pull it and you go up. And so on. Just watch the way they work while

I'm flying her and you'll soon get the hang of it. When you want to turn, turn the wheel like an automobile." They were using Deperdussin controls at that time. "You drive a car, don't you?"

Henderson nodded. His apprehension had vanished, charmed away by the sheer practicalness of the plane itself. Hitherto, he had only seen these strange monsters dismembered in a class room, or swooping birdlike and mysterious far in the sky. Now, observed close at hand, a relation between the thing and its function—its quality of a machine—became apparent.

The worn leather bucket-seat had received him comfortably; the metal cowling rose companionably about his shoulders. There were grease marks along the side of the fuselage, scrapings of sand on the cockpit flooring, a rubbed look where other hands than his had gripped the wheel. Obviously, this was only a workaday instrument, after all: it had flown before and it would fly again.

"All right," the instructor was saying. "This first hop I'll just take you around the course once or twice, and then when I wiggle the stick I'll let you fly her. Watch my arms for signals what to do, and when

I wiggle the stick again, give her back to me right away. Let's go."

They went waddling out toward the open water; then, cutting the gun, the instructor let her swing round into the wind. As she nosed into it, there was a raking blast from the motor as the throttle went full on, and they began moving straight down the bay, ploddingly at first and then more swiftly, with the waves pounding ever more savagely against the pontoon, the spray dashing higher over the wings: then suddenly it was as if the plane had found its equilibrium, as if it had at last discovered the effortless track.

The plane had come up on the step of the pontoon: the hammering of the waves died down, the spray vanished, and they were rushing expectantly forward, the plane itself giving slight taut quiverings as of gladness; and it had burst in on Henderson with an apocalyptic force that even this smooth swift joyous progress was not to be all. It was to be no more than the severing of a skin-sheath as, knifelike, he plunged into a new element, the air!

There had been, then, the wash-board surface of the bay, fifty—a hundred—two hundred feet below him, the masts of yawls at the yacht club anchorage sticking up spike-like, a motorboat seemingly stationary among its ripples, and the warm sun simmering softly over everything. Five hundred feet, and the plane had canted over steeply, the left wing pointing, like a rocket-stick tipping down at the top of its trajectory, toward a tiny dory far below.

Henderson glanced sharply for reassurance at the leather-clad shoulders and head of Ensign Weil, immobile in the cockpit before him, but slowly the earth and the sea swung back into place again—only now Fire Island and the reach of ocean beyond were on his right, and the hangars, squatting behind their strip of yellow beach, lay just under the left wing-tip. He understood that they had turned, and were making back up the course again. Ahead, the wireless towers at Islip had reared their gaunt heads and were stalking slowly toward him.

But the brilliance, the freshness of it: the air how elastic and unhindering, the sun how bright, the motor how competent and loud! The world was an enormous crystal, and he in the midst of it—above him the sky cupping down to meet, in a purple welding at the horizon, the green earth and the flashing waters that curved up beneath and around him: the whole great

91

ball sparkling and reflecting its sparklings in infinite reverberations of light—and he in the midst of it, drifting dreamlike, unattainable and secure.

It was at this moment that he observed the stick waggling vigorously—the signal for him to take the controls. He seized them, held them gingerly, and waited in a kind of still panic for what might happen next.

But miraculously, wonderfully, nothing happened. Like a well-broken horse that knows its way and follows it without guidance, the plane beat patiently onward; and Henderson, like a timid schoolboy at the reins, hardly dared move a muscle for fear it might bolt on him. A moment more and he was relaxing slightly, gaining confidence, when the instructor waved his arm toward the left—the signal for a left turn.

Instantly, his mind was all confusion, and he sat scanning the scattered fragments of his class room information, searching for the precept that would aid him now. He must rudder into side slips, keep the nose down and the engine tappets level with the horizon; he must watch the altimeter, push the stick hard forward when he wanted to take off, but what must he do when he wanted to turn? Like an admonition, clearly spoken, the answer presented itself to him: "Use the wheel like an automobile." Hastily, he yanked it around a half turn to the left, and almost immediately he knew he had done something wrong.

Even the mildest horse slows, stumbles, and turns its head on receiving an unintelligible command. So the plane: as if puzzled, its nose lifted inquiringly, the motor faltered and blundered and the wind-whine in the wires grew fainter; there was a slackening everywhere. Then, abruptly, it took the bit in its teeth, bucked once, whirled, and dived.

Earth and water made one dizzying lopsided revolution beneath him—and all at the same time rising, swaying and falling swiftly away again with the mad unreasonableness of waves—then he felt the stick shaking vigorously in his hands and released his grip: the instructor had taken control, and Henderson sat watching in wild bewilderment while the world swung once more in a retching circle, then settled like a spinning saucer, level but blurred, and in that blur he heard the wires' shriek rising higher, felt the wind tugging at his forehead, knifing his ears, and (he in that instant dying) saw the hard blue surface of the water rising with the speed of dread to engulf him.

Even as he watched, however, the nose of the plane came up slowly, climbing the level ladder of the water until it met the horizon-line again and (the wind's scream lessening, the propellor again taking up its beat) Henderson saw the instructor turning, the same sad frown on his face: he shouted something unintelligible and waved an arm.

It was not till they had landed that Henderson learned what his error had been. In turning the control wheel as one would that of an automobile, he had canted the plane's wings down toward the left, but he had failed to kick his rudder bar over at the same time and thus complete the proper manoeuvre for a left turn. More, like most beginners, he had pulled back the wheel as he turned it, thus elevating the nose of the plane and forcing it into a stall.

The result had been that it had fallen off to the left and into a tailspin, from which Ensign Weil, by the most expert management, had rescued it only just in time.

But Henderson had learned that one can meet death, coming suddenly, in a state of such bewilderment and confusion that the mind is occupied not with the effect of what is happening, but with the Why of it, and death, the event itself, is quite outdone.

He died three times. The third time he died was when he was living in France, in the little Norman village of Giverny, and one day he had started alone, by bicycle, to join a group of friends who were camping on the coast near Étretat. The whole incident was very odd.

He had left the town of Vernon, following the Rouen road, and, pedalling slowly, had fallen into that blank timeless reverie which the rhythm and the silence of cycling alone can produce, when he heard a motor car approaching at terrific speed down the road behind him.

Dutifully, he drew off to the side of the road to make room for the other's passage but even as he did so, and without glancing around, his ears told him that the motor car—sounding no horn but coming at express train speed—was bearing directly down upon him.

A moment later and he dared not look: there could be no doubt about it, the motor car, instead of swerving out to the left to avoid him, was still hugging the right side of the road, and he (inescapably now) precisely in its path. With a kind of numb resignation, he hunched his shoulders, closed his eyes on the brilliant world and (he in that instant dying) waited for the blow that would demolish him.

It came like a clap of thunder—and passed, leaving him undamaged and amazed. He opened his eyes, to behold the explanation.

It turned out that the vehicle approaching so rapidly behind him had been in very fact an express train—the Paris-Havre express. It turned out that its tracks, scarcely noticed by him until now, followed along the motor road and only a few yards to the right of it. Remember too that in France most railroads still cling to the Continental order, their trains passing to the left of each other, though motor traffic now passes to the right; and so it turned out that, in drawing off to the side of the road, he had only brought himself closer to the train which, traveling on the left-hand or nearest track and so separated from him only by a few feet of embankment, he now saw clicking briskly past. The testimony of his ears, and his own wild interpretation of it in the tumultuous moment, had done the rest.

But Henderson had learned that death, coming suddenly, can be met with a kind of panic patience that numbs the senses, so that life is paralyzed before it ceases, and death itself is quite outdone.

He died four times. But the fourth time he died is not to be related yet. Let us instead return to the day of his birth.

This was the sixth of April in the year 1897, and the event itself was perhaps a kind of death. For is it not in that moment that the inevitable process begins by which (as by decay: as a thousand substances— dead leaves, beetle-bodies, worms and worm casts, roots, spears of grass, flower petals, parts of the burial casket, bits of bone, or flesh, or nerve tissue, the body's blood—all rotting together, end as the common substance of the soil) so man's infinite potentialities, the qualities that make him momentous and unpredictable, are one by one worn down and pulverized, dissolved together until they merge at last with the homogeneous pulp of life?

Or: say that at birth the child possesses a thousand selves; that he has capacities, and stirrings within him to motivate them, that might impel him in any one of a thousand directions. Then, one by one, they are pared away, sloughed off, lost as if by accident or by the smooth pressure of life's flowing are dislodged, swept away, submerged—killed off, one by one—until in the end there remains only that thin pitiful remnant which represents not ourselves, but what our fate has left us of ourselves.

Then, only then, may a man look at himself as in a mirror and see *himself*—himself as the survivor: as a gaunt castaway, bare-boned and straggle-bearded, worn down to the ultimate thread of being, might stare with dulled eyes into a mirror and see himself as the sole survivor of some gallant company that had set forth on a brave sea-enterprise and had met with shipwreck and disaster. Then, perhaps, is the moment of death—but has not death been the process, and this death but its consummation?

So it was with Henderson. It is years since I have seen him, and now there is no knowing what has become of him. For even then, when I saw him, I had always the sense that he was several: that like the crowd that has not yet chosen its leader and begun its movement toward an elected goal, he had not yet compacted himself, not taken his ultimate direction. That, like the crowd, he might split apart, divide and subdivide, as it were disperse himself until in very multiplicity he had vanished before my eyes.

He like a crowd and himself lost in the crowd: I would see him (or was it he, so quickly disappearing?) and his eye like a burnt match as, pausing by the newsstand in Union Square; I would see him (or was it he?) moving with bent apologetic shoulders; or among the straggling legs on the Bowery, his hand touching mine; or glancing up and he (but was it he?) from the bus-top staring piercingly. Even then, when I saw him, I had always the sense that he was several: that it was always a subtly different Henderson who presented himself, or a different aspect of the personality that I recognized as his. Even then, the city would come between.

Or were they not all linked together? Were not all these others part of him, as he a part of them: his actions complementing their actions, as his life—in the vast life of the city—interweaving with theirs?

I have often thought that I might reach his end as surely (and perhaps my own as well) by following any stranger seen along the city's streets.

Henderson: it is years since I have seen him. My present occupation is that of a book reviewer, but I live in the country. At regular intervals I go to the city. Often, as my train draws on toward White Plains, I glance out my window and watch, through the gathering dusk, the motor cars spinning along the highway which at that point runs parallel to the railway tracks. I wonder if in one of them it may not be Henderson who sits, hands gripping the steering wheel, foot pressed hard on the accelerator, eyes scanning the road ahead, his whole being bent on reaching the city by seven o'clock—or, at the latest, seven-fifteen.

Then the lights inside the train are switched on, the brakeman passes along the aisle; ahead I hear the hauling heave of the engine. The green plush, the mahogany-tinted metal, the personages in the car cards no more real than my fellow-passengers nodding morosely over their newspapers—all become present in my mind.

Outside the window, the world is suddenly dark.

The Journey Down

The journey down that day was filled with incident. Almost even as he left the house, and: swinging the merest fraction wide on the curve at Evans's (beyond (he knew) the red barn the white house at Rehack's impassively awaiting his coming) he was confronted by a farmhand stepping erect and stiff along the side of the dirt road.

Nothing happened: he cramped the wheel in a little and went by with room to spare but as he passed the man turned his head solemnly to stare at him and (instantly) the meeting became portentous. The man's very glance foretold disaster.

Henderson knew (the man knew: "Killed, was he?" he might be (already expecting) saying tonight at Boerum's store. "I seen him goin' by 'saftnoon-time; like to run me down, he did." He had come stepping like a sentry, erect and stiff: behind him lay encamped the hostile future, waiting silently. As if he had heard the alarm raised, the signal given, Henderson knew (he knew) that in that instant his fate had begun its march on him: he knew) he had released the gas for a moment as he swung the car to clear. That infinitesimal delay (perhaps) had been the final correction needed to bring him, somewhere, at some time, squarely in the path of the instrument of his destruction, even now (somewhere) started on its unalterable course.

But nothing happened: thenceforward the old road, lolling lazily in the sunshine, received him benevolently, each turning passing him gently on to the next, and the next (where the man in brown overalls, his arm holding the brush hook upraised never to fall as, on) to the next, and down to Giddings' Garage and (taking the curve adroitly: the weight of the Ford flowing forward as pure momentum, as) releasing the clutch and (setting the inside wheels down in the gravel, the outer wheels braced against the camber of the road and) hauling her out of the turn again with a touch of the gas and up the grade and around down into Sherman and:

Nothing happened: the Grange shrugged its high

102

shoulders over him; Boerum's store sat placidly. There were the icy-white houses rising stalagmite-like in the sunlight. There were two girls (walking: in the sunlight, fragile) as if painted on glass in their yellow dresses against the green lawn. There were the trees dragging long whisperings through his hair as he (passing underneath; he) came dropping down into the town: the two girls the white houses the old man on his shaded porch peering (at him, impersonally) as at an aviator goggled helmeted in his cockpit, flying low.

Nothing happened: until at Judd's barn suddenly (at the wave of a magician's hand (high above him a man's legs: cradled in sunlight and (gleaming, the yellow cascade. Stolidly) the two horses and) materializing on the empty road: suddenly) a wagon-load of hay, blindingly in the sunlight menacing him.

Then motion leaped crackling all around him. He saw the driver rising sawing the reins scattering the paired team into fragments as the horses jerked startled in the harness and the man on top of the load staring scaredly grinning. His spine crawled up his coat collar as (the tires sputtering in the gravel) he rammed the car down in the ditch and yanked it up

again, his front fender rearing snakelike to strike
at the off horse's foreleg but swerving, missing. Nothing happened: he got by.

He heard the voice of one of the men trailing
scramblingly chokingly after him. He was already
halfway up the hill and settling into the climb.

Long ago when I went to West High School;
long ago when I had no thought ever of owning
a car of my own; long, long ago when I was a
boy in Rochester another boy took a crowd of
us out in the family's Packard for a ride in
Genesee Park and as we wound through the cin-
dered drives I observed a trick he had of setting
his wheel for a turn ahead and then twisting
about with ostentatious unconcern to talk with
the rest of us back in the tonneau while the huge
car nosed its way, as if unguided, obediently
around the curve.

I envied him, and when we also came to own
a car I set myself—undeterred by the difficulties,
undismayed by the dangers of the task—to
emulate him. I may say, too, that I succeeded;
even now, I take a quiet pride in the fact that I

rarely have to correct my wheel when once I've set it for a curve.

I abhor ostentation, however, and never turn around to talk with those in the rear seat.

(*All this a point to mention when interviewing someone about a job?*)

So: coming up with the speed of an avenger on the little blue sedan. Honking. Passing:

So: to the slanting turn at Haviland Hollow and, slowly: down the sloping spiral. Dangerous, but the Ford heels, then settles comfortably back into its springs again:

So: the whirr of the tread on the burled surface of the macadam. Two miles: THE ELMS:

So: we are now entering historic Route 22, full of cars hurrying purposefully

to PATTERSON 4 M.
PAWLING 9 M. BREW-
STER 11 M. WHITE
PLAINS 37 M. NEW
YORK 52 M. We are on our
way:

DOANSBURG
BREWSTER 5

BREWSTER
CROTON FALLS 4

CROTON FALLS
PURDY'S 3

PURDY'S
GOLDEN'S BRIDGE 4

GOLDEN'S BRIDGE
KATONAH 4

At thirty-five: the Ford runs loosely, easily. Little unexpected rattlings develop and disappear—a thrumming of the windshield frame against its post, a chatter from the rear bumper, a momentary ringing of a brake rod beneath the right front fender. Be not alarmed. Consider rather that now, in its leisurely

106

licit progress, the car is merely taking advantage of an opportunity to sound out and test each part. The Ford moves down the highway like a man strolling smiling, feeling the flexing of his muscles, while his hands in his trouser pockets jingling keys and coins.

At forty: everything is hushed, the machinery (the motor working contentedly under the hood the clutch plates whirling locked in an indissoluble embrace the transmission gears churning blithely in the oil the differential like a fat spider indefatigably weaving its intricate web of motion under the car and: all) spinning effortlessly driving the car onward.

At forty-five: a most welcome moan overtakes the motor—an aeolian voice that accompanies it thenceforward, urging speed.

At fifty: the Ford squats closer to the roadway; as if electrically, one senses the motor-thrust running tinglingly out to the very tips of the spokes to the tires brushing magnetically against the asphalt. The springs seem to flex more easily; it is even as if they anticipated obstacles; like a ski-runner gliding with bent knees the car planes skilfully over inequalities, smoothing to one gentle undulation the dip-rise-dip of a culvert. The scenery begins to blur. Trees are seen as if in motion: twigs and small branches are carried away. Considerable reduction of sail is necessary, even with wind quartering.

At fifty-five: the wind whoops past the windshield. Slight structural damage occurs (chimney pots and slates removed, hoardings demolished, branches of trees broken off). Ships must run under close-reefed sail, or lie hove to under storm sail.

At sixty: whole gale, with wide damage. Roofs of buildings removed, the buildings themselves often carried away or demolished. Trees uprooted. No sail can stand, even when running.

Above seventy-five: hurricane.

SHARP CURVE
SLOW

DANGER
CATTLE CROSSING 100 YDS.

HILL

One lends one's self entirely to the road,
following these dips and curvets, these deft
gambades, with attention but with delight

—as an inexperienced but enthusiastic dancer, his eyes alight and his coat-tails flying, might be whirling and capering, striving to match his steps to the steps of his incredibly graceful companion.

He lends himself to the dance: hair rumpled, cheeks flushed, eyes rapt and watchful, he surveys and would imitate her delicate swayings, her swift retreats.

She flees, he pursues: his eyes ever riveted to her face, brown-brightly smiling, whose glance yet ever eludes his own. She turns, he follows: clinging close to her, ecstatically aware of (her thrusting cajolingly. Sinuously, in supple swooping withdrawals, her) tawny young body pressed ever to his.

Headlong, the dancers: things flash past fast; the (trees dizzyingly, and screened behind them (sitting benched on their terraces, the (complacent chaperones: comfortably watching, the) houses green-earringed (and, quivering at a nod) their windows hung with jewels. The telephone poles saw stiffly away; the wires hum their tune, while) turning the green lawns the tapestried meadows, slowly and far: far beyond them the sky (the immense ball-room, its ceiling) glittering mirror-like, marbled with clouds: the) horizon line, low-running, alone keeping pace with them.

CONCRETE ENDS
500 FT.

One can look about now with a long neck, in this sun, this bright free air: his head, lightened by the warm breeze, rising balloon-like over the level landscape. One can light a cigarette and, as the rush of speed slackens, feel the world overtaking him—the barns, the dwellings, the fields that had been stretched rubberbandlike in their effort to keep pace with him now gently contracting on themselves, settling into solidity around him again.

CHAPPAQUA
PLEASANTVILLE 4

Nothing happened: but a fat man behind a lawn mower vehemently charging up the slope of a terraced lawn, and:

110

PLEASANTVILLE
HAWTHORNE 3

Nothing happened: but a man in a brown suit, carrying a brief case and coming briskly professionally down the porch steps, and glancing up and his eye meeting mine and:

HAWTHORNE
ELMSFORD 11

Nothing happened: but a long brown frown from the old frame building on the corner and the trees drooping sorrowfully over the insubstantial houses; at the curb a lone horse, doggedly dragging E. F. JACKSON GROCERS rapidly backward, and the lady in the Hoover apron with simple dignity behind her hedge, and:

111

He (jumbling them all together and (like tearing up old documents—not caring whether or not they are important—into fragments for a paper chase, and) carelessly: he) flung them over his shoulder to scatter swirling behind him. Nothing happened. The towns dropped away. No one took up the trail.

PONTIAC SALES
FLATS FIXED
GAS & OIL

REFRESHMENTS
HOT DOGS
CHICKEN DINNER

Nothing happened: but still that dark flavor of malevolence in the air: he remembered (stepping sentry-like out of the future) the farm-hand, his glance foretelling disaster.

So: ELMSFORD
ARDSLEY 3

112

So: RIGHT TURNS TO RIGHT
OF NO TURNING ON

(dustily the (speckled with lettering: the) yellow)

TRAFFIC TOWER RED LIGHT

So: STOP LOOK LISTEN
R.R.
CROSSING

So: SAW MILL RIVER PARKWAY
SPEED LIMIT
35 MILES

PASSING
NO
LANE
ONE

One has but to sit back
and watch the car ahead.

So: one mile like another mile. Whippingly,
the long thong of concrete, and the motor cars
scurrying screaming.

So: one mile like another mile. He, passing

113

and being passed: the old Oakland struggling whimpering—the green Plymouth roadster coming up behind it, and (but cautiously, as if to sniff the air) nosing out, then spurting to pass it—he passing the Plymouth—the Lincoln sedan looming suddenly on his left and (the big black body cradled luxuriously in the bright nickeled bumpers: the little leather aprons under its fenders dangling derisively as) traveling undeviatingly past him.

So: one mile like another mile, and up the rise and over the bridge and around and on, still climbing gently, while below and to the right he saw the red brick and yellow brick houses of Yonkers tesselating the hillside, and the declining sun throwing handfuls of birdshot to shatter the window panes.

(Through a parting of the trees ahead, he caught a glimpse, fleeting as in a dream, of the city's towers standing frail against the sky.)

This is how accidents happen: you judge wrong. The motorist approaching a curve must immediately and unerringly solve an equation among whose factors are the following: the camber of the road and the character of its surface (whether concrete, macadam or asphalt); the radius of the curve; the weight of his car and the distribution of that weight, sprung and unsprung; its length of wheelbase and width of tread; the diameter of its wheels; its speed. The rest is algebra.

What, then, when a motorist departs from the accepted formula, boldly ignoring its solution?

Henderson saw the car, entering the wide slow curve from one end as he entered it from the other. A white-painted line, shining and inflexible as a scimitar, defined the lanes the two must follow. It was a problem so simple that one could ignore it: operating on concentric arcs, the two cars could never meet. They would pass (at arm's length perhaps, but they *must* pass) one continuing northward toward its unknown destination, Henderson's going on to New York.

But suddenly (and his alarmed eye: had the dark sentry at last entrapped him? With an effect fateful and inhuman, suddenly) he saw the other car leave its course and (he bewilderedly watching: this car, by god or devil driven, flouting all man-made laws—its tires already sneeringly shearing the sacred line as) with the brusque assurance of the assassin it swerved to aim itself directly at him!

As when the man-of-war's man sees from his deck the approaching torpedo split the wave and cannot cry the alarm; as when the warrior, mute and motionless, watches the arrow sped or the knife descend, so Henderson—seeing the thick-snouted thing, inexorable as a machine on the scent, nosing toward him—sat transfixed.

For a moment only. Then, instinctively, his hand leaped to the horn-button on the steering post and the Ford—as an ass will in its helplessness, when in the jungle a tiger leaps—brayed a futile complaint.

It was enough. He saw the man (who had been drunk or dreaming: they were so close that he saw the man, his face and the terror on it. He saw the man) yank at his wheel, his face tilted in terror: then the cars sheered off and away.

Nothing had happened: he got by. But to Henderson (and fear and elation, mingling) it was as if he had at last encountered the ambuscade that Fate had laid for him and had won through unscathed. The purpose now was: flight.

So: swiftly, across the flats to Rumsey Road and

along down and (dribbling himself right-left-right through the side streets to Caryl Avenue (where, undulating like a roller coaster and) down to Broadway. Luckily the light was green, and) now with hardly more than a mile to go: dartingly, through the lazily-moving traffic.

A few minutes later, like a spent runner entering the gate of a beleaguered city, he passed beneath the Subway terminal at 242nd Street. He was in New York.

Macombs Dam Bridge Revisited

Here, where like some vast starfish drying in a (future) sun, he thought: the bridge (he thought) shall I carry it carefully home with me and put it on the mantel-piece; and stare at it, emblem of my childhood?

Here, where all hurrying, and only I standing staring down at the glum-glittering Harlem, slipperily its waters and (the oarsmen, still (practising for what races? Still, and the bright-colored jerseys, the brittle arms stretching) in their sculls lazily jerk-streaking the (waters: rippling elliptically, the) waters: only lips lacking as (with whispered apologies) the waters going sidling past the barges piled with bricks, and the tug boat with its fierce brown-bearded prow backing belligerently out into the stream. Distantly, all this remembering, and) the genial whiteness of the youngsters swimming off the farther shore. It is all so close to me that I dare not shut my eyes.

I dare not, here (where my childhood (like some vast starfish, he thought) in all directions around me) but if only one might go blindly back into the past:

Go down Seventh Avenue, and there again Gordon Houston and Bill Schultz whistling under the window; and there again the vacant lots behind the Interborough car barns where the gangs with their bonfires and I on my roller skates scooting scaredly past. There again the wide avenue dusty dusky in the evening and each shop window shooting out its glare, and I walking; and the girls skipping rope on the sidewalk and I watching; and the older girls in the apartment house entrances with their young men murmuring unimaginable somethings to each other, the girls going in groups of three or four and pulling and teasing one another and laughing themselves silly over secret jokes of their own; and I walking, watching. To re-create those crowds again. To lose myself therein.

119

Go up the Harlem River Speedway, and there
no motor cars but only Sunday silence every
day and the nursemaids sitting stiffly beside
their baby carriages; there again an occasional
trotter stepping briskly by and the sulky slickly
spinning; and the Elevated yards with the lines
of empty cars mournfully on the rusty tracks.
And there the river, silently, and there the High
Bridge lonely and magnificent in its airy isola-
tion; there again the sunlight falling unshadowed on the grass. To re-discover—to drop
back, gently, into—the cavernous silences of a
boy's mind.

Go eastward across the bridge, and there
where the bridge forks again to look down at the
park playground beneath: there if it were dusk
would I see again what once I saw?

Dusk, and the playground deserted, but
on the tennis courts three Irish kids—two
boys and a girl—engaged in a boisterous
rough-house, they laughing and mauling
her, she scurrying sometimes and sometimes turning and pummeling them but

laughing too at a good stroke as hard as they.

One had a piece of broom handle and was circling around behind her trying to catch it beneath her skirt. "Grab her head, Eddie," he was yelling. "Let's get her skirts up."

"Keep your God damned hands to yourself," she retorted, turning to face him, and then the other boy snatching at her: "I bet she's got pink ribbons on her pants," but she running backward out of reach. She, boldly, replying: "Sure. Come back here tonight and I'll show you." It was then that, glancing up, she noticed me watching them.

"Hey, look at the red head!" she cried. "Hey, Red! You want a piece too?"

Her voice, flauntingly, and her face flaring with excitement; and the sense of her, hot and challenging, down there in the dusk. And I shriveled by fear and wonderment: hurrying away.

121

To feel again the fear, the wonderment of the boy observing the world. To walk back across the bridge and up the causeway toward Edgecombe Heights, pausing at every dozen steps to look down over the railing at the scenes below: at the Manhattan Casino, its black tarred roof sinister beneath the bridge's shadow; at women leaning out tenement windows, creakily pulling in clothes lines; at men in shirt sleeves or undershirts stirring shiftlessly about in dim fourth-floor bedrooms, and I by the bridge's height made tall enough to penetrate their privacy. At boys playing catch in vacant lots. At men and women coming and going, pausing, greeting each other: hurrying along the streets below. To feel again youth's un-understandingness, the sense of being life's waif. To alleviate it by standing at the bridge's railing, poring over a world one may observe, but can not share.

To make my way home again, slowly, along the bridge: the pendant tenements, the strewn streets below—in the deep dusk, waterlike—the shadowy reflections of my loneliness. And on down Edgecombe Avenue, home.

"Those were the lonely years," he (thought, remembering: the curve of Edgecombe Avenue sharpening the edge of the bluff that dropped steeply down to a strip of park space and then Bradhurst Avenue and the ranked red brick houses of Harlem below and beyond: remembering (the ladies airing themselves in the hour before dinner on the benches along the cliff railing, and the children, made shrill by the threat of darkness, playing in the street. "I knew none of them," he said. "I knew no one except Theodore Gabriel whose father was an English gentleman in reduced circumstances who was our janitor and who did little plaster medallions of Woodrow Wilson and other famous presidents and tried unsuccessfully to sell them, and Theodore had no bicycle and my bicycle was often my only consolation," he said, remembering (the imitation marble stairs leading up to the apartment on the third floor, and then the still, dry smell of the long hall, and then the drop light with its shade of hammered brass and green-veined glass that hung suspended by four grotesquely massive chains over the dining room table where his father sat reading evenings. "I was fifteen," he said, "when we moved there from Seventh Avenue where we had lived before, and I knew no one. I would sit for hours by the window in the darkened parlor after dinner filled with what sadness no one—not even I myself—can now imagine. I would sit staring out at the lighted windows of Bradhurst Avenue down below and the tangled illumination thrown up by the criss-crossing streets beyond but what I really saw no one —not even I myself—can now imagine," he said, re-membering) far over all the roof-tops the P for Proctor's and the twinkling outline of the Dutchwoman on the animated Dutch Cleanser sign at One Hundred and Twenty-fifth Street and the club in her hand endlessly rising and falling against the night. "Saturday was the worst time," he said. "Youth has its pride and its observances. I was the new boy who went to a different school than the others and no one spoke to me and I spoke to no one. Saturdays I would get out my bicycle. I had a tennis racket in a plaid canvas case, and this I would hang over the handle bar. I would ride importantly away as if to a lively engagement at the courts. But the tennis racket was only a symbol: I had no engagement with anyone. Instead, I would go cycling aimlessly about the streets

only returning when dusk fell and it was time for me
to take up my vigil at the parlor window," he said,
remembering) the long slow slope of Convent Avenue
one could coast down almost to One Hundred and
Twenty-fifth Street, and the blank dusty streets of
the Bronx too wide for their traffic and empty-
seeming, where so many Saturdays, pedaling listlessly. "I was fifteen," he said. "And I knew no one.
There was a dark boy with a Spanish name, Cortez I
think, who asked me to play cross-tag with a bunch
of the others once but I think it was only to bedevil
me for he bullied me so that it was not long before we
were fighting. And once I found in our letter box a
letter addressed to me. It was one of those chain letters which command you under fear of the most hor-
rible penalties to send copies to seven other persons.
I did not have even so many as seven friends but I
made one copy and dropped it—unsigned like the
one I had received—in the letter box of a girl living
in the apartment house next door whom I had admired though I had never spoken to her nor she to
me," he) said; and (as, the waters, lip-lapping: the
gulls, their button heads alertly between their wings,

careening: the tug boat, broad fierce-bearded valiant, headed now upstream. And now the bridge (turning, and (ponderously. And warning bells ringing: the bridge-tender marshaling the trucks the motor cars all halting muttering, as) now the continuous line of the railings suddenly parting, the asphalt roadway the car tracks the sidewalk he would have traversed now severed in mid-air and sliding mazingly past each other, as) pivoting slowly on its center: the bridge, its length now only a passageway between emptiness and emptiness, swinging in a wide half-circle out over the stream, and) at his feet the water, suddenly nakedly, flowing.

It was like farewell.

But he, and (turning, reluctantly (like the bridge turning: this division in the way I would go? And) remembering: "The fear, the wonderment," he said. "The loneliness of the adolescent, life locked within him and he still locked away from life, but his body from its depths informing him that soon a new gesture will be expected of him. His watchfulness, his uncertainty, waiting for the meaning of the gesture to be revealed to him. His wanderings, and the things seen on his wanderings flowing past him like a river. Those were the lonely years," he said. "But I had the bridge to carry me over them," he said, and) he:

Turning to go.

The Cries of Old New York

All too soon the journey ended and (the young man his eyes clicking ratchet-like: as with a surprising unanimity (everyone: the girl with the pink hat the little man in the corner seat the gray the (smugly the fawn-colored top-coat, the) stout lady discontentedly the stout man. You would have seen) everyone arising crowding to (the doors rubberly sliding, to) the platform and) the car swept suddenly bare: only LUDEN'S Little Doctor in UNEEDA Candy Form Maiden Form REMember Formamint For Me WHO smiling their bright imperative smiles. It really does whiten the teeth!

But the girl with the pink hat, her legs vanish deliciously up the EXIT TO MADISON AVENUE, and: all the others briskly (as if on the deck of an ocean liner (the long planked walk the iron handrail the stiff steel stanchions, as) their volleying footsteps briskly) marching to East Side Subway QUEENS. Thinly, through the clamor (re-echoing bluntly)

128

winking pinkly over everybody's head the long-drawn
syllables:

> Follow the red line.
> Who'll follow, follow?
> Follow the long red line?

A cry age-old in its lilting cadences but the man
with the clicking eyes raspingly on the platform:
"Listen, friends. I am organizing a revolution," but
the crowd hurrying. No voices: only the stertorous
breathing of the tunnel (deep distantly: and) the
feet trampling, the street-rumblings dropping like
black stalactites from the roof: and (voicelessly, singing always) twinklingly:

> Smoking is prohibited,
> Spitting is unlawful.
> Warning: Do not lean
> Over edge of platform.

A stout man a stout discontented lady entered the
car, and a girl in a pink hat, smugly the man in the
fawn-colored top-coat: a little man scurried for the
seat in the corner. Suddenly (like an apparition: is
it Henderson in the doorway and the doors rubberly

closing? His hands clutching, his eyes brassy and)
the young man gesticulating:

"Does this train go to Seventy-second Street?"
The man leaning against the enameled post inside the
door shook his head.

"Does it go downtown?" The man leaning against
the enameled post inside the door shook his head.

Baffled, the young man (still staring bewilderedly:
he) ceased his efforts to enter the car.

The train drew out.

Someone laughed. The man leaning against the
enameled post inside the door permitted himself a
wise quiet smile but (still staring out the window at
the swiftly retreating darkness: he) did not turn
around. It had been the girl in the pink hat who had
laughed. Still no voices: no word was spoken or was
needed, but a feeling of warmth and intimacy spread
through the car; the gentlemen smiled and gazed with
less circumspection at her (delicious) legs. The journey ended all too soon.

"I am organizing a revolution!" but (voicelessly)
it was May Day; it was Fair Day, and all the Mor-
ris dancers skipping down the green line as (over the

feet beating: gaily the tune and) brightly:

> Next train—
>> Arrow to the left.
> Next train—
>> Arrow to the right.
> Watch your step
>> Getting on and off trains.

"I am organizing a revolution!"

The stout the (discontented and) smugly the fawn-colored top-coat and the little man the girl in the pink hat: all (startled) looking up from their morning-afternoon (tomorrow's) Daily News; and he (his eyes buzzing, his bared teeth, his stabbing forefinger: he) rising addressing them.

It was the first time a voice had been heard there in years.

"I am organizing a revolution." And then, continuing more didactically: "As distinguished from merely revolving. Don't you ever get tired of whirling round and round? Don't you ever weary of going back and forth?"

Like a sausage in its skin the car in the tunnel, and the young man (his eyes auscultating each quivering breast in turn: solemnly, he) said: "I am going to tell you a story. I had a friend who went round and round—a friend who went back and forth.

"A charming chap. You would have liked him, if you had seen him making his way here and there. From Times Square to Grand Central, from Grand Central to Times Square. Going back and forth through the city—making his way in the financial world too.

"But something went wrong inside him—here," placing his hand dramatically on his heart. "He got the idea that he was being followed—more, that it was himself who was following him!

"I shall not attempt to describe to you the devices he adopted in the attempt to shake off his pursuer. All were unavailing. Turn as he might, speed as he might, the dread huntsman still remained on his trail.

"Soon, the pace grew too hot for him. More, it was at about this point that he took to writing letters to himself. 'Poison pen' missives. Letters filled with the direst secrets—secrets which he had believed no one but himself could know. From here to blackmail was but a step: the end came rapidly.

"One morning (and by an ironic coincidence it was the morning of the day on which he was to marry the president's daughter and be made a member of the firm) he received a letter, demanding that a certain sum of money be delivered at a designated spot, or the most damaging disclosures would be made. The sum demanded was far more than he possessed."

The narrator paused. By now, the stout lady was sniffling, the stout man wiping his spectacles, the girl in the pink hat openly in tears. The train was drawing into Times Square (or was it Grand Central?) station.

"That was the end," the young man continuing, inexorably. "Packing a few belongings, leaving a hasty note, he vanished, his life forever blasted!" But the train (and the doors, rubberly sliding as) halting. Everyone arising, crowding; and he: "An old legend has it that his ghost still rides, back and forth and back again, in the shuttle train.

"Ladies and gentlemen, I am—," but the feet beating; deafeningly the feet and the beat defeating him:

The journey had ended all too soon.

I saw him last on the platform, but (above the: hurrying) above him winking the (gaily) tune:

> . . . the red line.
> Who'll follow, follow?
> Follow the long red line?

And he (clutching, and an old man. He) was saying: "I have a friend who is insane, and his delusion is that he is insane. What course of treatment would you advise, sir?"

But the old man, embarrassedly.

Voices at Union Square

There are (every day there (are there?) are) there
every day tens of, I mean hundreds of, thousands
THOUSANDS of (men women: hurrying, the tall
man the fat woman grayly (the face as if crackling,
and) the two and in shawls. He has a long nose rooting
in a brownish beard and all (hurrying) their feet
freckling the sidewalk. It is like a boardwalk: the
Coney Island glitter of an ORANGE PINEAPPLE
DRINK stand and across the street the open park
space (ocean-like) dilates the air (odorless but for
the (but more like jelly, tremblingly, the)
pink shirt-waist perfume; and yellow, as,) pausing by the Subway the news stand the sleek
pale young man, but (his eye like a burnt match, as)
everyone: the men the (women?) men) women hurrying past the windows belching BARGAIN $100,
000.00 CLOSING OUT ENTIRE STOCK BIG
SALE SILK HOSE SPECIAL FORCED TO
SELL TO MOVE TO CUT PRICES IN HALF:
BIG SALE AT F. & W. GRAND 5—10—25—50¢

—74¢—86¢—99¢—$1.09—$1.34 is too much. Let's go see what they have at Klein's MONEY BACK within FIVE DAYS.

"Take it easy ladies plenny a time."

"How much is that Art Lovers Camera Studies I'll take a Collier's." The pale young man has bought a Collier's, and GITCHA wuyds of all song hits: pretzels three fa five but he turns away and (egglike the three men slowly walking talking earnestly, and) the man in the blue suit: the man with the lady (smugly) in the fur coat. Stepping down from the curbstone he turns his (derby hat turns his) head with ostentatious elegance and spits on the side away from his fair companion, and: the four girls skittering chattering:

"Cmon Mae—"

"Ah Huyman's awriyut. Ssa nice guy—"

"Elissen Mae wadja Ma say wen ya cmin lass niyut?"

(She had said: "You listen to me Mary no daughter a mine's gonna stay out to four o'clock in a mornin it beats me where you get such ways after the bringin up I've gave you—," she going on and on

136

and the girl, her ears as if glazed, wearily not listening):

"Less get a cross a street ssa guy follin us—"

"*Wad she say Mae?*"

"Ah, she juss about buynd up but I din pay no attention—"

And (like peanut brittle laughing) chattering, and the sleek young man, his eye like a burnt match (but a spark gleaming):

"*Cmon Mae—*"

Or you can JOIN the NAVY. You can TRAVEL. You can LEARN a TRADE. Looking out in (like into a funnel: distantly) the park sun-bolstered and there where a man on the pedestal of the George Washington statue and the little crowd raveling around him. He waves his arms but it is all (in the redundant air) as if miles away, and his voice splintering in the screech of the Broadway-4th Ave. trolleys (one after another: rounding the corner) around the corner. After their passing the tracks lie, worn but smiling, gazing placidly up at the sun.

There is a lesson there; and high over the roofs the Consolidated Gas Company has hung a Doric temple like a picture on the wall: a picture too high for one to reach to straighten it and it is swaying. There is a lesson there.

There is a lesson in that sudden silence when the red light halts the cross-town traffic, and the Painless Dentist sign peering down from the second-story window sees only four girls chattering, glancing back and laughing, crossing the drained-empty street; and a pale young man, houndlike grinning, following them.

There is a lesson there for you and for me, but (you on the boardwalk sidewalk) you are hurrying. You hurry your way. I'll hurry my way. I am hurrying after that (is it Henderson? That) man with the burned-out eye and the thin sleek face: he is following those girls and the girls are splitting up at the corner. One going one way and the other the other way, and the fat girl is standing there, waiting for the lights to change.

("*Hello babe—*")

It was just as if he had dropped there; just as if slowly dropping out of the sky:

138

down past OLD GOLDS—

down past Ida's Beauty Parlor—

down past College OF BALL ROOM Dancing—

down past PROPPER'S Sample Shoes—

down past Chop Suey—

down past DIAMONDS—

down past Pineapple Drink—

—As if (as she afterward said) he had dropped right down out of the sky and there he was standing smiling where they all were standing watching her. (We had all been watching her. Maybe in a few years she would be too fat but now her legs were just plump enough beneath her blue skirt and her eyes glancing behind long lashes: now for two minutes (while the lights were red on Fourteenth Street) she would be beautiful. She ignored us). We watched her, and from up and down Fourth Avenue clicking shuttling past (like Time overtaking itself: in each a man with his watch in his hand and leaning anxiously forward) the taxicabs.

No man, no woman could hope to breast that current. Like a dainty maiden helpless at the river's brim she stood on the curbstone and he with his pale sleek smile his glowing eyes, beside her. Faintly, over the flowing street, came music from a radio store. The sky was blue. It was quarter to one by the Central Savings Bank clock, five minutes past by the Gas Company's. It was the time for love.

He smiled.

She smiled.

"Hello babe—"

Little girl, you're beautiful. You're NEAT. Your drowsy caterpillar eyes, lazily waving long lashes at me. Your conjuring lips and your nose, powdered white, like a little snow-mound between your china-red cheeks. You're SWEET. I like your loppy little hat. The bracelets at your elbow. The pink-and-white whoopee socks you wear on your FEET. You can't be BEAT. You're not too thin and you're not too fat. You've got me all in a HEAT. You're just my MEAT. Let's go take a bus-ride. An all-alone-with-us ride. Let's go to a movie or something.

"Cmon babe—"

(That was the last we saw of them: he squeezing her arm and guiding her across the street perhaps to

the Academy of Music Big Double Bill or the Tango
Dance Palace or perhaps to the Irving Place BUR-
LESK AS YOU LIKE IT as (the lights changing)
the clicking course of the taxis slowly halting: but)
I have discovered something. I will tell you or the
Editor of the *Mirror:* Dear Sir,

It is a small matter but I have discovered that it
is not Time overtaking itself as the taxis race up
Fourth Avenue but instead a loose manhole cover at
the corner of Fourteenth Street. It is a small matter
in itself but as each taxi reaches the corner and
swerves in to avoid the Car Stop standards its course
almost inevitably is such that one front wheel and
one rear wheel pass over this manhole cover, produc-
ing a sound which it is difficult to render phonetically
but which might be transcribed thus: "Kla-*kling*,
kla-*kling*."

It is a small matter but one which when kept up
too long can I assure you drive men mad and may
already have done so. Cannot the city keep its manhole covers in order?

125th Street Comic Strip

"Excuse me please I am looking," he said. The crowd slanted past him like rain water and he with bent apologetic shoulders: his caved chest holding his empty heart. Making his way toward Seventh Avenue.

1.

It's a long loud street; a (laughing, a) wide red mouth full open and (resplendently Herbert's Home of Diamonds: REGAL SHOES: Ideal COFFEE Pot: Howard's $22.50 Clothes: LINGERIE) all the shop windows gleaming like teeth, but teeth (in the clear impertinent Harlem air) so impeccably bright, so glitteringly even that you would almost never guess that they were false. No really Mrs. Yefkowitz it's a beautiful set and you wouldn't hardly ever guess.

It's a (laugh, a) street laughing, but the laugh

loud and insistent as when (at the Apollo BUR-
LESK Mid-Nite Show To-Nite) Joe Schnozzle
smacks Trixie Delisle right on her rear or rather as
when in the comic strips WHAM (riding down to
work in the subway every morning and home again
every evening and everybody looking over everybody's else's shoulders laughing: ZOWIE) Harold
Teen knocks Lilacs dizzy with a crack on the (BAM:
and "Tweet tweet" the little birdies as, looping, his)
jaw.

That was Mrs. Holtzmeyer just went into Weis-
becker's Market to get a today's special rib roast
29¢ the pound. She's a fine figure of a woman, always
a good word for everyone and she lives on a Hunnert
n Tent Street with a very nice apahtment beautifully
furnished even if it is a walk-up, all the ladies go there
Wensdys for the Radio Bridge Lesson but we need
not bother about her: did you see Abie The Agent in
yesterday's *Journal?* Isn't he a scream?

2.

But (he said, stopping me. "I'm in a hurry," I
said, but) let me tell you a funny one about Maxey

Lanke. You know Maxey, little thin fellow works out of Rehmer's real estate office, lives up on Morningside Heights. ("Excuse me please," and; but his insistence perspiring at me). Nice guy, good for a laugh any time you run acrost him, but it just seems him and his wife don't ever hit it off.

She's a little blonde, good-looking and a snappy dresser, but before she married Maxey she was a secertary in some office downtown, got around forty a week and always treated herself to the best, an now she don't see why bein married should hafta make her act any differnt. You know, a natural born spender.

Well, Maxey's generous enough, always free with his money, but every once in a while she wants a new fur coat or something, an then Maxey has to put his foot down an then there's arguments.

Well, the other night they're walkin down the line an she's been at him for weeks about how she wants to buy a new bridge lamp for the livin room an here she sees one in the window at Blumstein's just like what she wants, an only eight dollars or somethin like that. Only—get me?

Anyways, a bargain, the way she looks at it. So she

says it's now or never with her, an will he buy it or won't he? Well, Maxey's been in a game the night before an got took for a couple a sawbucks, so he tries to put the brakes on, an with that the trouble starts.

Well, it lasts so long, her bawlin him out an gettin louder an louder till finally Maxey gets embarassed, what with people beginnin to listen, so finally he gives her a little push, sort of, an then does she burn up!

"No man'll hit me twice," she says. "Once is enough," she says, "An from now on I'm through. From now on," she says, "I go my own way," an with that she starts off acrost the street, an no more does she step off a the curb when a taxi comes cruisin along an WHAM: it knocks her kickin.

Funny? ("I must be going I'm looking," I said). But you ought to hear Maxey tell it. He's a card, all right. Anything for a laugh, that's Maxey.

3.

All day the crowds (and at night the lights, the windows) go whistling laughing: and she (softly (in gray? And) the sonorous fingers, the healing eyes:

she, somewhere) among them. I am looking: but (the auctioneer beckoning to me, to you, to all of us: perched rooster-like behind his counter, crowing) NOW ladies n genlmn Um gonna hafta ask you ALL to kinely step down this way a little closah DOAN block a doorway I wancha ALL to see this beautiful TEA set all solid china in a famous cherry-blossom patten Um gonna offah fah sale to a highess biddah IF you wen to a depahtamint store to buy ut you would PAY from TWELVE to FOURTEEN dollahs for this same SET but tnight we gotta dispose a lot a muychandise I'll take any bid that's offahed me will you all please STEP down this way doan block a doorway PLEASE wat um I offahed for a tea set AND a gole wriss watch AND a crystal diamond ring AND a Mexican ruby necklace will somebody STYAHT a bidding? Will somebody say TWENNY dollahs will somebody say eighteen?

Will somebody say ONE dollah? ONE dollah I'm offahed will ya say TWO? ("Two," I say). THREE who'll say FOUR?

("Three-fifty," I say). FOUR Um bid are ya done are ya ALL done? Four dollahs ONCE. Four dollahs TWICE ("four-fifty," I say, and) SOLD. I am

buying all this for my Emily. She is plump and amiable: I met her at Manhattan Beach last summer and,
lying together on the sand and, dancing together:
cosily her body clinging to mine and, her wide red
mouth when she laughs and:

I love her. Or anyway I almost love her. I tell you
it's a funny thing but I can't take her serious and
you want to know why? It's because her Ma is always
calling her Emmie and I have to laugh because it re-
minds me of Moon Mullins. You know, in the News:
there's a Emmie there that runs the boarding house
where Moon lives. I told her once and did she burn
up? ZOWIE. Is that a laugh?

4.

Most trains stop at 125th Street. From the car
window you look down at the (grinning: like den-
tistry) the double line of lights. P is for Proctor's, and
pinkly wriggling the (far away: is it a) jewelry
store? You have a moment in which to meditate on the
adventure of sometime spending a night at the Hotel
Naomi. Then (with a shudder of axles turning)
the train starting: the street canting slowly backward

and (into darkness running) in every apartment-house window a pink-shaded lamp is burning.

Maybe you are going to Syracuse. Well, Syracuse is a nice town.

A Ballad of the Bowery

"It's very odd," he said, and I said, and he said: "It's very odd," but I was not listening to what he was saying. It was a strange wild night, with snow in Wisconsin, fog on the Lakes, in Indiana a keen wind whining in the telegraph wires, the wind slatting through empty freight cars in Oklahoma; rain in Ohio and rain in Delaware, and here on the Bowery (where (we were walking) we were (wading deeper: as taking buoyancy we were floating) swimming like fish in an evil river; and) the black night, flowing heavily. Dark shapes went winging past. Motor trucks, painted red and green, bloomed and faded. Taxis shiny as eels came nibbling along the curb; and the El like a broad-bellied alligator, waddling:

> —*It is nine o'clock.*
> —"Y'ever been in South America?"
> —It is half past four.
> —*I have no home.*

149

There came then (I am reciting) one of those moments when every impulse of the city's life seems suddenly stilled: when the whirling wheels of traffic, halting, coincide in a slot of silence; and the key turns; and a great door opens; and one feels that the next step will carry one over its threshold into unimaginable regions. I remember he was saying: "You know, it's very odd," he was saying. "But of all the streets in New York the only one where I've never been asked for a hand-out is right here on the Bowery." I remember looking about, and thinking that everyone around us must be dead. It was then that the man in the old brown reefer-jacket approached us. *"Cn ya spare me a dime gents, buy m'self a cup a coffee?"*

> —It is quarter to eight.
> —*It is ten o'clock.*
> —"I jist come in from Niagara Falls."
> —*I have no home.*

I am reciting every incident, but I shall not attempt to describe his whispering eyes, his mossy lips, the shoving way he had of walking, the ragged trousers that dribbled down his legs. His features even now are indistinct to me: then, they were illuminated as by the lightning flash, for an instant only, and in that flashing glimpse seen rather by the memory's eye than by the visual, and seen blurred—or as if his lineaments dissolving subtly changing even as I looked—so that his face was the face of someone, or anyone, or all, among all the friends I had once known and had forgotten. He stood planted before us (his hard hand out: words fumbling in his teeth) and I (knew I) had recognized him. I knew (I knew) him.

      —It is eleven o'clock.

      —"All they want is mechanics."

      —It is three o'clock.

      —I have no home.

Say, who are you anyway; are you Jim Butler, Craig Potter, Loring Staples? "*No.*" Did you ever live where I lived, in Buffalo, Denver, Rochester, New Haven? "*No.*" Tell me, who are you; are you Chuck Lakeman, Homer Fickett, Bob Shafer? "*No.*" But they all (the gray, the drowned purple: heaving, the jelly-fish face, the crab's eyes creeping: the men (I am reciting) all walking but (ropelike: the long lines of (men walking: men) twisting among the El pillars, unraveling at street corners, and) all together moving (walking: the men) like a long rope (crusty dripping: the hard-shell faces) dragged heavily up from the (black: the flowing: the) sea. They were all) walking: all the men walking and I had taken his hand: side by side we were walking.

> —It is ten past six.
> —"Thing is they don't feed y'enough."
> —*It is twelve o'clock.*
> —*I have no home.*

Shave 5¢ Haircut 10¢. *"Come along who wants a haircut."* Looking back I could see the other: "It's very odd," he was saying, and his white shirt-front, dapperly strolling. *"Come along":* we were walking. Long lines waiting at the Bowery Mission; lines at the Holy Name; lines at the Y.M.C.A. *"There's no place for us there."* Inside in a yellow sawdust room men were eating Pig's Knuckles Sauerkraut 20¢ Large Steak Jack's Style 25¢ Soup Spaghetti 5¢: in the People's 5—10—15—20¢ Restaurant the (men crouched over tables in (steaming the Coffee Pot: succulent smelling the) Quality Lunch where) men inside were gulpingly eating but we outside walking.

"Come along I know another place farther down."

>—*It is one o'clock.*
>—It is half past five.
>—*"I been in all them places."*
>—I have no home.

But wait, who are you? Tell me who you are. *"Come along I can't wait."* It was then (it was there (the other, dapperly strolling, rejoining me) at the corner of Hester Street I halted: glaring his crusted face but quivering: as if the rope tightening and (he was telling me but (the El train at that instant— rocking, rumbling—passing) drowning his voice in (blackly) the noise; and the long line moving) the men walking. I know not how or when he vanished (I am reciting every incident exactly as it occurred to me) or whether, indeed, a better explanation of his disappearance—and a less miraculous than that implied by the word "vanish"—might not be merely that, as (the lightning flash, fading) his fancied resemblance to some one among my half-forgotten friends, on closer inspection, became less apparent, it grew correspondingly more difficult to differentiate between him and the other men (walking aimlessly:

so he melted among them and, disappearing) cease-
lessly walking; and) we were walking: "That's the
first time a bum ever tried to pull a touch on me here,"
he was saying, and lifting a (wearily) hand; and the
taxi slacking, swerving alertly.

—*It is two o'clock.*
—"Time we were getting back uptown."
—*It is three o'clock.*
—I have no home.

Times Square: Portrait of a Man
Talking to Himself

Pick-ups go by twos and threes but the whores
walk alone—but those hissing eyes as she meaningfully beneath the awning and the rain simpering sug-
gestively. . . . A bad night to be a broad sister at
this hour when Time so limpingly—and tell me where
the snug room in this dripping darkness and where
the bed that still waits patiently for you and who,
me? . . . But all quiet now in LUCKY KRAM-
ER'S LUCKY SHOP where the snappy-looking
Neckwear 55¢ draped languidly over the ivory-
headed walking sticks and all dark as if forever dark
in the Gaiety Theatre—and in O.SAPORTA MUSIC
the tinkling symbolical ash trays wide-throated the
bellowing BARGAIN Victrolas and the huddled har-
monicas moanin' lower than cost 98¢. . . . Which
would you rather have—or would you prefer a china
lady tinted like life and engagingly clad in a jacket
just short enough not to reveal what are you talking

about? . . . Shall we buy a little lady—or maybe after all the one back there on the corner? . . . Or wouldn't it be more dignified—to stand on one of those little balconies over the windows of ADAMS HATS and watch the dawn patrolling the avenue? . . . But here I am talking to myself and I all alone except—suddenly the pale young man coming hound-like out of the idle darkness and his thin acid grin going smoothly over the flowering doughnuts in the window. . . . His eye like a burnt match—but a spark gleaming as he turns down Forty-fifth Street and on what scent disappearing? . . . At three A.M. all footsteps sound the same.

> (And he entering, and the other lying loosely on the couch: the other laying aside his True Detective and with a smirking amusement: "Hi, Henderson," and lazily watching. "Home from the wars, eh?"
>
> And he with his squeezed thin grin: "I'll say."
>
> "What'd she want?"
>
> "Oh, Christ! She don't know what she wants. I tell her I'll fix it to see a doctor and she don't want that. I make as if to slip her a double saw-buck and she don't want that. I know what she

wants, all right. She's sick of clerkin'. She wants
to marry me."

"Whew! Don't let her do that, boy."

He carefully hooking his dripping overcoat
over the closet door but, turning tentatively: "I
don't know. Mae ain't such a bad kid, y'know,"
and as if embarrassedly. "Jesus! I wish there
was a shot of gin in the place."

But the other, flipping open his True Detec-
tive again.)

At three A.M. all cities sound the same. . . . In the
yawning dawning the street a doomed emptiness and
the rain voicelessly inquiring—but from everywhere
but as if arising far far behind the jumbled rows of
buildings sleeping awkwardly in their ranks the
solemn mumbling that might be the musing roar of
London or the thick night-breathing of Chicago.
. . . Only now a Ninth Avenue El train coming
rambling interminably around the corners of the
years—and bringing with it all the way from the
Pont Neuf those nights when I would be walking
home toward the City-Hôtel and hearing the market
carts going rumbling over the deep-bellied bridge.

. . . Wonder why? I mean why the clop-clop of a horse's hooves deliberately declaring that what side-street how many blocks away in the slumbering Forties is that street in Buffalo one night when the rain thinning the skim-milk skies—or how long is it since Ping Byrne and I wandering down the Lungatevere and the buildings like these buildings with the night-sweat glistening greasily? . . . Thin as paper the pavement and "Tear here to open" along the dotted line as the quick-clicking heels perforating—but into what depths then dropping as the rain timidly asking what man is hurrying whither? . . . As he with bent apologetic shoulders—and his caved chest emptily. . . . He turning wearily down Forty-fourth Street?

(And he entering and, noiselessly, but from the darkened bedroom the woman creaking querulously: "Is that you, Henderson?"

"Yes, Emmie. It's me."

"Well. It seems to me you come home later every night instead of earlier. I swear to God I don't know what other woman would stand for it."

"I know. One of the Boston trucks broke a

158

spring up in the Bronx, so Mr. Crandall sent me along to check the load while they transferred to another one."

"Yes. Mr. Crandall. And you never have the nerve to say no to him, no matter what he sets you to do. Why don't you tell him you got a wife home, sometime?"

"I know."

"God knows it's no fun for me, this kind of a life. I went to the pictures and there was a fellow there that was trying all the time to make me. If I'd known what time you was coming home I might of gone out and had some fun with him."

She from the darkness remorselessly adding sentence by sentence and he still standing holding his glistening hat as if he didn't know what to do with it, and then suddenly the heavy coughing like deep waves enveloping him.

"Yes, and you in this rain and all. You'll be laid up with your chest again, and then where will your job be?")

But still the rain and silently stitching the tattered glowing each one separately—I mean how sadly

159

scatteredly now the few street lamps here where at midnight a vast incandescence. . . . At midnight the lights sprinkling like springele and candy-coating with blue yellow and sugary pink the indigestible sky—at midnight the hurrying faces cobbled bobbing and the lights for each one an individual luster. . . . But not now when the sky in dark solitude and the framework of a quenched electric sign a skeleton grinning wordlessly—not now when the whole square withdrawn in emptiness and the street lamps plucking the silence one by one. . . . Not now not now or ever—but let X mark the spot. . . . Where in a forest of petrified NO PARKING KEEP PEDESTRIANS PASS LEFT OR CROSS HERE NO ONE RIGHT WAY PARKING—thick fell the arrows and fierce the combat where in the iron jungle the two great avenues crossed swords at last. . . . And the rows of little steel disks buttoning up the pavement—where you and you and how many of you died yesterday or was it tomorrow? . . . But not now when only the rain puckering the sidewalk—and I and . . . Dapperly the man and his white shirt front glinting as briskly around the corner and . . . Ink-winkingly—down Forty-third Street.

(He entering, and like a threadbare fabric the high thin (and tightly stretched: under the smoke-dusted lights, the) talking laughing; but through one of the holes of silence the host coming hurrying carrying highball glasses, but stopping unsteadily peering:

"Hello there, Henderson. Come on in, boy, you're just in time for a drink. Wish you'd been here earlier, though. We had—," but suddenly staring baffledly. "Why, what the hell! You *were* here earlier."

"Sure I was, Mannie. I just thought I'd go out and take the air, sort of."

"Yes, I know. But," and still bewilderedly: "I mean, last I saw you were *here*."

"You're right, Mannie. But then I thought I'd take a walk or something, so I went out and wandered around for a while."

But the other shaking his head stubbornly: "I don't get it. I mean, I could swear I just saw you come in that door."

And he laughing: "I can explain everything, Mannie. But how about that drink you were going to give me?")

161

Or suppose that all the radios in all the world were slowly to run down—like a phonograph mournfully in discords diminishing and descending. . . . Suppose that no one answered—but all walking unheeding past him when the Daily News Inquiring Reporter asking "Do you think our Navy should be reduced?" . . . If the hungry men were to be left groping helplessly for their hamburger sandwiches —as in all the All-Night Lunches the lights suddenly went out. . . . If the subway train had halted in the deepest tunnel—and the passengers sat staring at each other with inimical eyes. . . . Or suppose that in the motion picture theatre apprehension had given way to dread certainty—as it became apparent that not the villain but the smiling blond hero himself was to suffer death. . . . If one were to stand all day in the Grand Central station—watching the hasty good-byes being said among the piled-up suitcases. . . . And counting the tears that are even now being swept up by the sweepers their brushes skirmishing across the polished floor—if one could count the tears. . . . Or as when at Coney Island a sudden storm comes crashing in from the ocean and the boardwalk deserted the ferris wheel halted in its ponderous turning—if the crowds were to rush from the parks the amusement places and the excursion boats were to set out empty to sea. . . . Then I might find some cause for this causeless melancholy now invading me—then I might prick this bubble of remorse and release its aching vacancy. . . . I might understand this reasonless despair—but not here where I walking wearily and the long fingers of the dawn slowly hollowing out the sky but not now. . . . Not now while the rain insistently and the passive violence of the pavement—not here but the gaunt buildings sniveling and not now or ever while the night trailing sobbing down the endless avenue and I walking wearily. . . . Is it Henderson—that man in the worn brown overcoat hurrying down Forty-second Street? . . . At three A.M. all faces look the same.

TOPIC SENTENCES, III.

Perhaps It Was Henderson

Perhaps It Was Henderson

Often, I have loitered in the Grand Central Terminal for upwards of an hour, studying the books in Womrath's windows, the shirts in J. P. Carey's, the toys in Mendel's—postponing the moment when I must emerge, plunge in, walk onward. Often, I have nowhere to go.

Often, it seems I have no friends—or rather, I have friends, but all of them have Watkins, Algonquin or Stuyvesant telephone numbers and live in the Village. Tonight, I will have none of them. Tonight, I will follow strangers; they at least will not deceive me.

That man before me now, that man in the worn brown overcoat hurrying down Forty-second Street with an air of pre-occupation, glancing rarely to right or left: is it solely by chance that I find myself following him, in Indian file among these other thousands, as a man in the wilderness might follow his guide? Is not some fate involved, and will it not be the worse for me if I let him escape me?

Perhaps he is only going home to his dinner, in some apartment that will be reached by a journey on the Sixth Avenue Elevated, a descent to Columbus Avenue at 103rd Street, a walk of one block north and half a block west, and a climb of three flights up an imitation marble apartment house stairway. But perhaps that is the destination foreordained for me, as well.

He will hang his hat and his overcoat on the hatrack in the hall. He will pause in the kitchen doorway as his wife, her face glistening with a mixture of sweat and steam from her cooking, glances up perfunctorily from the gas range. There will be no welcome in her eyes, and no surprise. She will merely note that, as expected, he is there. "I thought I would get supper early," she will say. "So we could go to the movies after. It's all ready to go on the table," she will say. "The spareribs and sauerkraut that you like."

He will sit down and eat, beneath the drop-light with its shade of hammered brass and green-veined glass that hangs suspended by four grotesquely massive chains over the dining room table: the hard bright light glittering on his knife as he cuts the meat and on his fork as he lifts it to his mouth, the light moulding his face in ridged shadows as his jaws chew, and making his hands look flimsy and old as he reaches out across the table for the potatoes or for a slice of bread. His wife will be sitting opposite him, eating.

"There's a Janet Gaynor at the Audubon," she will say. "If we could get there in time."

"I'm sort of tired tonight. The way they got the stock arranged down there now there's an awful lot of running around you have to do."

"I know," she will say. Then, more animatedly: "I bet there's something you never noticed. I got a man that would fix your arm chair today. I was up on Amsterdam Avenue to the market and I saw this little furniture store so I went in and asked. And the man come right down with me and looked at it, and then right after he sent a couple of boys down to take it away. He said it would be done in three or four days. But I bet you never even noticed it was gone."

"No, I never noticed," he will say, turning obligingly to stare into the darkened front room. "How much did he want?"

"Four and a half," she will say. "He wanted five. He's going to cover it with blue velvet and fix the

169

springs too. That other place wanted six, remember?"

"I know."

"Wait," she will say, rising from the table. "I got a pineapple pie from Cushman's. Wait till I get it."

And he, waiting motionless save for his jaws still chewing, he motionless in the hard bright glare like a rabbit trapped in the beam of a flashlight: perhaps a feeling of wonderment will have enveloped him. The worn leather cushion on the seat of the rickety wire-stayed chair he uses in the stock room; the easy chair in the parlor, its sagging springs, its frayed covering—these bear his impress, they are in some way connected with his history. Janet Gaynor at the Audubon—the men, soberly importantly, filing past the ticket window; the wives waiting at one side, decorously uxorious in the ornate lobby. "Five dollars": the furniture man glancing up shrewdly, and his wife: "Why, I wouldn't think of paying more than four." "Well, say four-fifty."

All these in some way factors of himself, evidences of himself, existing—as if a judge had called on him for proof and he had answered, "Yes. Go to the furniture store. You will see my name on the ledgers there;

my chair, worn by the weight of my body. Go to the Audubon Theatre. The girl in the ticket booth will not remember me, perhaps, nor will the ticket taker at the door, for he sees so many like me. But I remember them, and can describe them."

He sitting motionless as if trapped in the circle of light, while his wife in the kitchen getting down plates from the shelves for the pineapple pie: "Ah, God!" he will be thinking. "Why am I here, and how did I come this way?"

And tonight, after the movies, he will lie in his bed in that mood of ungrateful contentment which comes from having accepted less than one wanted of life, and which is assuaged only by dreams.

Perhaps he is Henderson. I have not seen his face; I only catch a glimpse of a pale cheek and a thin flat jaw in the glancing light as he leads me past Stern's windows. He stops at the news stand under the Elevated stairs, buys an *Evening Journal*, and then (and with such haste that one might think he fled me) runs hurriedly up the stairs and vanishes.

I do not hinder him, though I had him trapped for an instant. I had him cornered, there at the foot of the Elevated stairs. I might have hailed him, stopped him; by my assurance of manner, by the adroitness of my questioning, I might have convinced him either that I was a friend of his youth or a confidence man. In the latter instance, he would have called a policeman; in the former, we would have gone off together arm in arm: in either case, events unprecedented in both our lives would have followed.

Instead—like the hunter who, seeing the rabbit sitting immobile and defenseless in the beam of his flashlight, is moved by a moment of pity and holds his fire—I let him go.

Perhaps he is Henderson. Or one morning when driving down, and at Pleasantville there was a man in a brown suit carrying a brief case coming briskly professionally down the porch steps of a (brick-winking, the) slant-roofed bungalow: down the concrete sidewalk toward me as I driving past and glancing up and (as if he had been expecting me: as if he would climb in the seat beside me and direct me toward a new destination) his eye meeting mine.

The feeling of understanding behind that level gaze: the feeling that he could lead me, would I but follow.

Or: one spring evening early, I was walking down Fifth Avenue, the night just darkening and the innumerable lights as if wistfully in the (twilight and, dimly: a lady (the white brow leaning; falling the (leaves, the) fingers falling and softly (a song? Dying the day and) in the twilight a lady) is seated at the piano. I was walking down Fifth Avenue, and all the office windows prematurely lighted, like jewels million-faceted now in the) twilight, diamonding the air. Suddenly, a bus drew up to the curb and halted beside me.

There was in its appearance an effect of the miraculous, an instant appositeness as if it had come in answer to a prayer: the bus (its green sides shell-like glittering, rebuffing the outer world, and within (so separately, through the windows) the condensed illumination crowding the (rattan, the seat backs, the neat noses, the filed-off faces facing forward. As if enclosing a denser air, the light limiting the) miniature interior: the bus) resplendent and theatrical, like a machine from which a god might spring.

And then glancing up and seeing the man on the bus-top (but his face scoured of all expression, even the features as if scrubbed away by the white light of the street lamp, and like a halo, but: the man on the bus-top, his eyes) gazing piercingly into mine.

Then a bell ringing, a clogged clanking and the motor roar as (melancholy as a ship vanishing at sea, the dwindling windows) the bus moving heavily onward up the avenue, and he riding; and the sense that the encounter had been significant: that somewhere, somehow, our fates would be again involved. I did not follow him, but wherever I walked that night his white face moved above me, like a white brush-stroke edging the panorama of the city.

Once, too, coming home late at night from a walk in the downtown sections of the city, I entered a subway station to find it deserted.

It was a local stop—Canal Street or Franklin— and the news stand was glassed in, locked and untenanted; the ticket agent drowsed; only the faintest and most distant rumblings came from the mouth of the tunnel. I walked listlessly up and down the platform like a visitor in some abandoned museum, staring at the slot machines, the posters, the vacant benches, as such a one might regard the relics of a civilisation thus doubly dead.

And then, suddenly, the empty platform was invaded! A party of men and women—a dozen or more, and all chattering, laughing: the women's sharp heels clicking smartly on the concrete, their brilliant dresses foaming out beneath their wraps; the men hurrying from one to the other as if in some intricate dance, the men making gallant gestures and the women smiling, nodding their careful coiffures—a party of men and women appeared: the men's deeper voices weaving in with the women's high merriment and filling the station with an indescribable bright jollity.

I cannot tell you how amazed I was, and how uplifted! Where had they come from? I had been walking down Varick Street, and then across to Hudson and so to Greenwich and Washington, and then zigzagging through the tangle of side-streets: all had seemed dark, deserted—and yet in some one of those silent houses these happy strangers had been having their festivity!

I moved closer to them, affecting an air of nonchalance (though, indeed—except when some lady's quick glance, as she turned from one gentleman to another, traversed my face almost unseeingly—they took no more notice of me than might a host of angels

175

of a mortal) but their conversation gave no clue to the mystery: in fact, as I soon discovered, they were speaking Swedish, or some other of the lilting Scandinavian tongues. A local, as if it had been awaiting their arrival, came into the station soon after.

I rode uptown with them as far as Times Square, watching them avidly but not enviously—feeling that, that night, I had shared a dozen lives.

Perhaps Henderson was among them. I could not see all their faces plain.

But indeed, are not all our lives in the city made up of such incidents as these? How often, seeing some nocturnal figure slipping, furtive and anonymous, among the dark shops, the silent houses, have you not wondered whither he is hurrying and what his errand —wondered, even, if it may not be a friend, masked from you by the night and his own dark purpose! How often, walking homeward late at night and seeing one high window still alight, have you not paused staring, wondering what went on behind the curtains, on what scene of kindliness or cruelty, of passion, joy or wrath, that light shone!

In the room (perhaps) the silence buzzing angry

and unnoticed, and the two men facing each other; and the mirror staring through and beyond them, frankly interested only in the opposite wall.

In the room the two men facing each other: the one speaking swiftly, scatteredly, and the other watching unheeding, as if behind the sweating words of his adversary he heard some calmer, more momentous adjuration; and then the speaker pausing as if he too had heard the voice of doom, and the look of startled hopelessness in his eyes: he in the round revealing moment staring motionless, and the other saying almost abstractedly, "I told you I'd made up my mind," and like a grim corroboration the bursting blast of the pistol-shot.

Perhaps (in the room) a man alone, and moving restlessly: restlessly his hands moving among the clutter on the mantel-piece, his hands picking up the dull bronze dancing figure and then setting it down, and then his eye meeting the eye of his image in the mirror and he for a moment staring: as a gaunt castaway might stare with dulled eyes into the mirror he staring, seeing himself as the pitiful survivor after shipwreck and disaster. And then (perhaps) slowly striding to the open window and looking down at the converging lines of the building beneath him, at the whole swift falling away of the façade; and then (slowly, confidently) leaning out against the breast of Fate: and the long rush downward.

Then, perhaps, the telephone ringing, ringing unanswered.

Then, perhaps, the knocking at the door.

Then, below on the anvil pavement, the crushed and bleeding body, the limbs dreadfully awry, the wide eyes empty and from the staved-in chest one last moan escaping—the body smashed by the hammer blows of height, and the clotted crowd hungrily staring.

I passed soon after.

Perhaps it was Henderson. Or: sitting one hot summer night on a roof-top on Fifteenth Street, overlooking Stuyvesant Square, and the night a vast twinkling intermingling of far stars and even more distant-seeming skyscraper windows; trees and tree shadows and the shadows of strollers moving in the park space below, whence the cool scent of voices rising above the slow subsidence of the day's heat; and suddenly (while the others all talking, saying: "I can't read Longfellow, isn't it a pity?" Saying: "My idea has always been, when I get to be about fifty and want to retire somewhere, to go live in Corsica, say at Ile-Rousse." Saying: "What we've got to do is be ruder to people we don't like." All talking and saying: and I, suddenly) seeing a light flash on in a window in the dark block of houses facing us across the park.

The feeling (have you never known it?) that the light was friendly: that if I crossed to that doorway, rang that bell, I should be warmly welcomed. That the light was a summons, requiring me to answer it. That someone was in that room who awaited my coming.

Perhaps it was Henderson. He would be waiting at the head of the stairs to greet me as I came up, and then hauling me into the room (where the piano gleaming satiny, volubly the brown armchair; and the books on the shelves watching solemn silent attentive, while he) wresting my coat away and ("Here, let me take your coat. Sit over there," and) with that wrangling affectionateness that was always his manner: "What do you say to a drink, now? What'll you have?"

But that was another time, and that meeting was

destined never to be accomplished, for when at last I rang his doorbell, climbed his stairs, it was too late. Meantime, much had happened, that summer. Indeed, it was at about this time, or perhaps somewhat earlier, that I had had a rather surprising interview with his wife.

Helen Henderson was a slight, brown-eyed and brown-haired girl—not pretty exactly, but with an air of freshness and vivacity that gave her charm. Or perhaps it was really the sense of neatness about her—the almost desperate neatness, say, of a child in its Sunday dress—that made her appealing.

For in her, as in the child, one felt that it was largely make-believe. She would fold her hands and eye you gravely. She would sit primly facing you, with her skirt drawn demurely down over her knees and in even her flimsiest evening gown a suggestion as of starch and careful laundering, and you would not quite believe it. As with the child in Sunday dress, you would feel that somewhere within that armor of decorum there was a live lithe little body, with quick active legs and a heart hotly beating, only waiting to be let loose again. You felt that all her prim compactness was only assumed for the moment:

that there was a yieldingness behind it that would some day take another impress and a warm passion that eventually would overflow its restraint.

But I never came to know her very well. It was Henderson whom I saw most of, and him only rarely in casual encounters about town. On the occasion of which I speak, I had dropped in at the Patterson's, who were having a party, and was mildly surprised to find her present there, though Henderson was not. In fact, I believe I made some comment about it— "Where's your husband?" or something of the sort —and she turned her bright impeccable glance to me. "Oh, I'm on the loose tonight," she said.

Shortly afterward, she brought her highball glass over to the corner of the room where I was sitting, and with that casualness which we all affected at the time, seated herself on my lap. "D'you mind?" she demanded lightly, and then drew her head back, bird-like, in an oddly attractive way she had, the better to inspect me. "Because I want to talk to you," she said. "About Henderson."

"What about him?" I asked.

She still stared at me, but now more seriously. "Well, he thinks so much of you," she said. "I thought maybe you could do something with him. Have you seen him lately?"

"No, I haven't," I admitted. "I never seem to run across him anywhere, any more. But then I come down to town so seldom now, in the summer. What's the matter with him?"

She had propped one elbow on her knee and now, opening the hand thus uplifted, she balanced her glass on the flattened palm and eyed it thoughtfully. "He's got a new girl, you know," she said, as if in an aside. "I thought you'd have heard about it."

I hadn't, at that time, and I was honestly amazed. I said as much. "Well, you will," she assured me with a kind of weary fatalism. "He's all over town with her, these days. He's crazy," she said, still addressing her attention to the glass, and then fell silent for a while. I felt that shock of slightly panicky bewilderment which sudden confidences often inspire in one and could say nothing either, but at last I stirred a little and then she turned and confronted me, and I saw that her eyes were glittering with tears. "I suppose you think it's none of my business," she said.

There was a kind of valiant hopelessness in her voice that was infinitely touching. After all, according to the code of married freedom that we all subscribed to, it *was* none of her business what her husband was up to, and I recognized the price in pride her confession had cost her. "I don't know who else's business it would be," I assured her warmly. "No, it's just that I'm so surprised. I thought you two got along so well together."

"I thought so too," she said. "It's sort of a surprise to me too," she said, but even while she tried to smile at that, tears began trickling miserably down her cheeks. "It's nothing to weep about anyway, is it?" she asked, still desperately smiling, but a moment later she reached blindly past me to the table beside my chair, dropped her glass there, and then hid her head against my chest. "Don't let anybody see me," I heard her saying muffledly. "Don't say anything to me for a minute and I'll be all right."

I held her and said nothing. No one saw her. Rugs had been kicked back in the corner near the phonograph and a few couples were dancing, and strewn about on the couches and the chairs were other couples variously entangled. Smoke spun slowly in the air and the room had a teetering feeling, as if the noise and the lights and the music, warring together, had set it swinging. I held her like a sacrifice to this gayety, stared solemnly, and said nothing. Once someone called to us across the room, and once a man whom I didn't know paused swaying before us, peered, and then as if he realized he had penetrated into a soberer air, turned and almost tiptoed away. I held her and said nothing: indeed, I thought, there was little I could say. In a minute or two she raised her head again and, dry-eyed, offered me a little shameface smile. "Silly!" she exclaimed. "I don't know what's the matter with me. Will you hand me my glass?" And I handed her her glass.

She took a drink from it and then, still perched on my knee, produced her compact and busied herself in repairing her make-up. "And it really isn't any of my business," she went on, with an air of extreme common sense, as she powdered her nose. "We always agreed we wouldn't try to hang onto each other in case—well, in case anything like this happened. I thought you knew all about it or I wouldn't have mentioned it.

"But he hasn't been quite fair about it, either. We promised we'd always tell each other, but I had to find this out for myself. There!" she said, and snap-

ping her compact shut she turned quite composedly
for my inspection. "Do I look all right?"

She was drawing her defenses in around her again,
and I felt that in a moment more she would be inaccessible to me, and yet now I wanted sincerely to
help her. "But look here," I began. "If you love him
there ought to be something we can do about it. How
do you know how serious this is?"

She eyed me almost defiantly. "If I love him," she
repeated. "That would be just my hard luck, wouldn't
it? It's whether he loves me that matters now, isn't it?

"No," she said. "I'm not worried about myself. I
can get along. I can go back into advertising again.
Or I think maybe I'll just chuck everything and take
a trip abroad. That'll give him a chance to make up
his mind—and besides, I can get my divorce there.
We've got to get this settled somehow," she said. "We
can't go on like this."

"You'd better wait a while," I said, but she shook
her head at me wordlessly and I saw that she was near
to tears again. "Who is the girl?" I asked hastily.
"Do I know her?"

"I don't think so," she said. "Unless you met her
last year when we lived out in Briarcliff. That awful

185

year, with us missing trains and raging over break-
fast and never getting the newspapers—I don't see
how you can like living out in the country. But I
thought it was all over with, until now this comes
along.

"She lives out there now," she said. "And that's
why he's making such a fool of himself—but that's
his business. But the funny thing is that I introduced him to her, or maybe these things always happen that way. Anyway, there was a bridge club out
there that Henderson teased me for joining, though
I had nothing in God's world else to do, and she was
in it, and so eventually we were all having dinner
back and forth. You know. And all the time this was
going on, I suppose."

"Oh, Lord! No," I protested. "I mean, I know
Henderson, and he wouldn't—"

"Well, it doesn't matter," she cut in. "But there
are all sorts of little things I remember, now that I
think back about it. Or I tell you when I really think
it started. There was one time this spring just after
we'd moved into town when they thought my father
was dying, and I had to rush up to Rochester for a
while; and it was after I came back that I noticed

him acting—well, I could tell. Or I could have told, if I'd stopped to think about it.

"But he *is* being such a fool," she said. "Because she's married too. She's married and she has two children, and she's older than he is to begin with, and I know she isn't really fond of Henderson at all. All it is, she gets bored living out there in the suburbs, and this is sort of fun for her. That's what makes me mad, really. I think I wouldn't mind so much if they were really desperately in love. It's the feeling that it isn't terribly important, even to him.

"It makes me think that I'm not important to him, either. But I really don't know what they think they're going to do. Can you imagine Henderson with two children suddenly thrust upon him? And there's her husband—he's one of those heavy possessive people, and crazy jealous of her, not like any of us at all. He might do anything, if he ever found out.

"Or maybe they really are in love with each other, after all," she said speculatively. "She's very pretty. Much prettier than I am, and bigger and more sort of—well, womanly, I suppose. I've always thought Henderson looked down on me a little, because I'm so small. As if I were a child and he was afraid he'd have

187

to take care of me—though God knows I've tried not to be dependent.

"But then you'd think, if they were really in love he'd want to tell me about it right away, so he could get rid of me as soon as possible. Wouldn't you?" But now I saw that she was only skating lightly over the surface of her thoughts. She was talking to me glibly, as if she were telling the story of two other lovers, whose fates did not concern hers. And now, as she turned to me with her question, she gave a little bounce of her body on my knee and surveyed me smilingly. "Well," she said. "Let's not talk about it any more, shall we? I'll go to Paris and have a fine time, and he can marry her, and everything will turn out swell. Can I have a little of your drink? I've finished mine."

But I was still urgently interested. We were all a little tight, I suppose, and I had had one of those flashing and comprehensive ideas which come, when one is in such a state, with the force of revelation. I started in to expound it at once.

"Listen, Helen," I said. "I'll tell you what I think. Instead of being too dependent on him, the trouble is you haven't been dependent enough. What I mean is,

you've left him too free, or you've made him think you
could get along too well without him, and the result
is that he's just cut loose. Or he hasn't cut loose, exactly—," but already I felt lost in the, it seemed,
immeasurable rightness of my idea. I could not see
why she didn't understand it as readily as I had. It
could not be expounded.

"What I mean is," I finished vaguely. "You ought
to give him more responsibility, instead of less. Make
him think he had to take care of you." And then I
went all to pieces. "Have a baby, even," I suggested.

"Have a baby!" she began, as if that capped the
absurdity, but then my very earnestness made her
pause. "Maybe you're right," she said, but only
kindly. "But it's too late now."

"Not if you love him," I began, but this time she
halted me.

"One of the things you learn when you get married," she told me, and I remember her intent brown
eyes peering at me with a curious small school-teacher
effect over the rim of her glass, "is that love isn't everything. There's your pride and his pride and—oh, all
sorts of things. You can't just throw yourself away.
There are some things you can't stand for, no matter

how much you love a person; in fact, that's the reason you shouldn't stand for them. I'd rather leave him feeling that he respected me than hang around him, trying to 'keep his love.' You can offer yourself, but the other person has to come forward to take you." But that was the end of her seriousness.

Perhaps she had come tacitly to the conclusion that nothing I might offer could be of help. Perhaps the very burden of the problem had become wearisome to her and she wanted, above all else, to be rid of it for the moment. Or perhaps the course of the drama, and her part in it, had long ago been clearly settled in her mind and she felt that this small scene, as an incident in its unfolding, had run on long enough. At any rate, she glanced about with a definite air of having done with the subject, and then her eye fell on a girl across the room and she gave a little cry. "Why, there's Ann Honeycutt!" she exclaimed. "And I haven't seen her for ages. Here, this is your glass. You'd better take it. I must run over and say hello to her."

I seized her as one might seize a bird about to take flight. "But listen," I pleaded. "What do you want me to do about it?"

190

She glanced back at me, and I perceived from her manner that she had quite forgotten what her original request had been. "Oh, help pick up the pieces," she said, and then turned back and smiled a little ruefully. "I didn't mean that," she said. "You've been nice, just even listening to me. But you know how it is. There isn't anything anybody can do—now. Just see that he doesn't make too much of a fool of himself, I suppose."

And then she was gone, and soon after I learned that she had indeed sailed for France, ostensibly for a summer's vacation. I have sometimes wondered if I were not, in some part, responsible for that—if my blundering opposition on that night when first the idea presented itself to her had not in itself supplied the pressure needed to indurate it firmly in her mind.

But then, those were tangled times, that summer: I found much to distract me on my visits to the city. I was intensely interested in Miss Elizabeth Godwin of Roslyn, L. I., a young lady whom I had never seen, but whose name and a specimen of whose handwriting —"Marlboro, America's finest cigarette"—confronted me from the seat-back before me whenever I rode on a Fifth Avenue bus.

I was worried, too, about Little Orphan Annie, who had gotten herself lost again, and this time so thoroughly that it seemed that Daddy Warbucks might never find her; and there was a young man on the Chesterfield ads whose tired eyes met mine with a look of such utter hopelessness, as he raised them from his littered desk and announced, "I'm working and smoking overtime. Hence a *milder* cigarette," that I felt an almost personal responsibility for his plight.

I was filled with concern, as well, for a window demonstrator I had observed in a drug store at the corner of Lexington Avenue and Fifty-ninth Street who removed imaginary corns from a plaster foot with an indescribable elegance, and tapped the pane arrestingly, and flourished his pointer and traced out the words on the placard announcing a large trial offer—only to see the crowd on the sidewalk, at the conclusion of his demonstration, turn coldly ungratefully away.

Always, so far, he had begun all over again, undismayed, but I wondered what would happen to him

—and, indeed, to all of us—when, as some day they must, his patience flagged and his enthusiasm finally expired. The Hands of Death moved slowly around their clock-face in the Daily News, pointing at last to 'Guns, 232' and 'Autos, 576'—a not unusual position in so great a city as New York, but for some reason to me an awesome one. I waited, wondering when my turn to add a digit to one or the other of those figures would come.

Then, too, there was Henderson—but already I had realized that he was slipping away from me. Have you never, in the city, gone through a period when it seemed that the intricate mechanism of circumstance which governs your relations with your friends had had its cycle altered or its rhythm disturbed, so that for a time your movements no longer coincided with theirs?

So it was with Henderson: where once our paths had led us toward frequent chance encounters, I seemed fated now to be always just ahead of or just behind him. I would telephone his office—only to find that he had not yet arrived there. Phoning again later, I would learn that he had come in meanwhile but had been urgently called away.

"Henderson has just been here," I would be told on arriving for cocktails at a friend's apartment, or I would leave the party, as I might learn later, only a minute or two before he in his turn appeared. A taxicab would flash past, as I walking, and a face be seen inside it—to be lost again so swiftly in the hurry of traffic that it was impossible to know whether or not it had indeed been he; and often, turning down some familiar street, I would be informed as if by an aroma in the air that I had crossed his trail again, but too late to take up the scent. "Mister Henderson was here till no more than an hour ago," Tim would tell me as I approached the bar of the little speakeasy we both frequented. "Had a bit of a load on too, he did. Not that he wasn't well-behaved, though, for he always is that."

"Did he say where he was going?" I would ask.

"No, he did not. He was asking for you, too." And I would be left to meditate on the mysteries of that vast clock-work, the city, and to wonder at the incalculable elements of its functioning that had prompted this emergence, and yet had timed it so cunningly as to leave no clue to the causes that lay behind it. Where had he come from, coming here, I would be wondering; where had he gone, and how could I now overtake him?

At some time, too, during the period I speak of, he arose at a drunken party and delivered a most extraordinary harangue. But then, the whole incident was peculiar.

I had come upon him, I remember, quite unexpectedly at the home of an acquaintance: he was leaning against the wall by the radio cabinet, tinkling the ice in his empty highball glass, his expression stiff and abstracted.

"I didn't know you knew the Tishmans," I remarked in surprise.

"I don't. Who the hell are they?"

"Why, they're the people that live here."

"Well, let's get out of here, then. I don't like the name."

"But how'd you get here, though?"

I remember that he gazed at me wryly, slyly. "Lecture tour," he answered cryptically, and then raising his hand he suddenly bellowed: "Ladies and gentlemen! Will you *please* be quiet? Did you ever hear the story of Will West, the Negro who looked alike? Did you ever hear of Will West, who was jailed in the year nineteen-three at Fort Leavenworth, Kansas, and found that there was another Will West—just like him in every respect and even in all the Bertillon measurements—already in the pen there, waiting for him?

"I am here to tell you the story of Will West and how it affects our daily lives. Will you *please* be quiet?" People in those days were ready for anything, and in all the faces that had been turned toward him surprise melted quickly into laughter. Someone cried, "Hear! Hear!" and others cheered and applauded. Henderson joined his finger-tips together in pedagogic fashion and regarded his audience solemnly. It was a favorite role of his.

"But the case of Will West," he went on. "Or, as I prefer to call him, the man who looked alike, need not detain us long. Though of prime importance to the student of anthropometry—and even, because of the peculiarly dramatic series of coincidences that surround it, of interest to the layman as well—it is not alone in the annals of dual identity.

"Indeed, if we look deeply enough into the subject, do we not find that we are all victims of double identity? Or, to confine myself to the pronouncements of

196

my own experience, let me say that I at least have found such to be the case.

"Not long ago, in the elevator which takes me to my daily work, an impulse which I will not attempt to define moved me to call out to the elevator boy 'Eleven' instead of 'Six'—the number of the floor on which the firm that employs me has its offices—and I think it not too much to say that the resulting experiences have altered the whole course of my life. Let me tell you what occurred.

"At first, as the elevator deposited me in what was unfamiliar territory, I was timid and even terrified. Then, emboldened, I looked about me. Perhaps you can picture my surprise when I tell you that all I saw there reproduced, in even the smallest particulars, the elevator lobby of my own offices, five floors below.

"There was the same floor of black-and-white tiled linoleum, the same paneled walls of brown-stained pine, and the same framed prints on the walls. There was the same ground-glass bowl hanging from the ceiling, and the same illumination flowing with scientific indirection down from it over everything. And behind the information desk sat a girl with the same lacquered countenance and the same expression of polite disdain. There was but one thing to do, and I did it. Summoning what courage I could, I approached her. 'Is there a man named Henderson here?' I asked.

She nodded. 'Oo wansa see'm?' she inquired, in a *patois* that I recognized.

" 'Oo wansa see'm?' she asked again, for I give you my word that in that moment I could not speak. I could only stare at her. *I* was Henderson—but *was* I Henderson? For Henderson was *here*—and then *who* was I? I felt that I needed, above all, to gain time. 'Whose offices are these?' I shot at her.

" 'Ssa a Dee-Lite Disappearin' Bed Company,' she shot right back and added, not to be deterred: 'Few wanna tell me oo wansa see Missr Henderson Ull senn in ya name.'

"It was but a step to the elevator bell, and I pressed it. I should have liked to inquire further into the meaning and uses of a disappearing bed, but by now the thing had gotten too much for me. And besides, in a way I felt that I—or that other I whose existence I had just discovered—ought to know all about that subject. A down-bound elevator stopped soon after.

"I escaped, and I have never gone back there again,

for who would deliberately come face to face with himself? I do not roam; I stay on the sixth floor where I belong, but often I look up from my desk toward the ceiling, and wonder what I am doing up there, five stories nearer the sky.

"It is an odd tale," he continued. "But nevertheless, I assure you, true. But indeed, are not all our lives in the city made up of such incidents as these? For instance, only yesterday I was walking through Washington Square when directly in my path I saw a ghostly message, white-lettered, scrawled on the pavement. It was written in chalk, as I discovered on examining it, which fact perhaps precludes the possibility of the miraculous, though the message was so apt to all my problems that I could almost believe it. At any rate, I copied it down on a piece of paper I had in my pocket and shall now, as a conclusion to this little talk, read the precious words aloud to you.

"They are as follows," and consulting a crumpled envelop, he intoned: " 'How shall we escape if we neglect our so great salvation? Are you saved God's way? If not, why not now? God-has-one-way-only.' The last five words," he explained, "were heavily underlined in the text, so I have ventured to emphasize them accordingly. The interpretation I leave to you."

He bowed and sat down, and the waves of the party's merriment swept over him, carrying him across the room and out of my sight. When, later, I sought for him, he had gone. It was well towards the autumn before I saw him again.

I had been hurrying up Seventh Avenue late one afternoon on some errand or other, as I remember, and I had just crossed Fifty-third Street when I happened to notice him.

There is—or was—a parking place in a vacant lot at that corner, and near its entrance and just at the edge of the sidewalk, a bootblack's stand. It was there that I saw him, sitting enthroned like some burlesque potentate under the green-and-yellow striped sun-umbrella that shaded the stand, and gazing out meditatively at the thoroughfare, while at his feet the bootblack knelt in suppliant fashion.

I called to him, and at the sound he started, but it was a moment before his eyes, swiftly scanning the scattered figures moving past him, discovered me. Have you never, hailing a friend encountered unex-pectedly on the city's streets, seen his gaze go blank and his expression stiffen in some unreadable emotion, as if his whole inner being had gone suddenly fixed and motionless, like an animal trapped in the beam of a hunter's flashlight?

So it was with Henderson: he for a moment crouching, peering startledly, and in that moment I was wondering: was it a look merely of surprise that had crossed his face? Or did it contain embarrassment and annoyance at thus being singled out, given a name, among the nameless numbers of the crowd? From what far journeyings of the mind had I recalled him, and might it not have been better if I had passed on silently, leaving him in solitude?

But then the moment passed: our glances met through the sifting faces, and he was greeting me delightedly.

"Jesus!" he cried with a frank amusement. "It's funny the way you pop up when you least expect you. And it's so long since I've seen you, too. But imagine finding you here!" And, seizing my hand, he hauled me willy-nilly up into the vacant chair beside him. "Come on up and have a shine."

I yielded awkwardly, vaguely demurring. "Still funnier, finding *you* here," I observed as I settled into the chair.

But at this he turned sharply toward me. "God! No," he protested, with a seriousness that was somehow ludicrous. "I'm here all the time," he said, and then eyed me mistrustfully as I laughed. "You don't know," he added, and turned away again.

I remember that there was a storage warehouse across the street and, faraway-looking through the hot sunlight, two men lazily unloading packing cases from a truck at the curb. Henderson watched their movements for a time. Then: "You know," he remarked. "If you'd come along a minute or two earlier, you'd have seen someone else who knows you. Laura Sennitt—remember who she is?"

"Yes, of course," I said. "She's the girl you brought out to see me that day in the country, isn't she? I liked her."

"She liked you too," he said, and I remember his voice even then as if from years ago, his voice almost too casually: "She always parks her car here when she comes to town. You know, she's afraid of traffic or something. That's why it's so funny your turning up here," he said. "I just saw her off a minute ago," he said. But I cannot remember all that he said.

I remember the heat that lay like a bright dust,

suspended in the air, and the sunlight a stinging haze through which the people walking: the sunlight quivering whitely on a man's hand swinging forward and then the hand shrinking to shadow again as it fell to his side. The man's hand swelling and fading as the man walking briskly past us down Seventh Avenue and I watching him, wondering if he knew what the sun was doing to his hand.

I remember the bootblack's polishing cloth snapping briskly and the smothering smell of the asphalt: the grimy street sounds and the brick walls rearing panels of heat around us I remember (and he suddenly hastily questioning: "But when'd you get down from the country?" he demanded. "Why haven't I seen you lately? Why don't you ever call me up?" But I cannot remember all that he said, remembering) his eyes slowly centering on mine, and in that glance an appeal and a justification: all our friendship in that glance but veiled (already) by a premonition of farewell. I knew so well what he was thinking.

Laura, he had said: this was where she parked her car when she drove down to see him. And, the brief meeting over, this was where they came when they said good-bye. There are times when the commonest object can take on an as it were symbolical glow, illuminating all around it with strange meanings, and I knew that this bootblack's stand, and the parking space behind it, had suddenly shown themselves as outposts, making visible to him the narrow boundaries of his empire over her, and defining as well that larger domain into which he could never enter: he had just seen her off a minute or two ago, he had said.

He had just seen her off a minute or two ago, and (still, perhaps, in his apartment the coiled spot among the pillows where her body lying nakedly: still, the red-stained cigarette butts lying crooked among his on the ash tray, and on the piano, mournfully, the two empty highball glasses. But she: driving off, and) perhaps running into a red light at Fifty-fourth Street. She had sat there waving her hand and making faces at him, and he waving back, and then the traffic started moving and she moving with it toward what destiny, or was she escaping? He would never know.

Others would see her, but he never, and her yellow hair glinting gallantly in the sun as she driving smartly up Riverside Drive and on into Westchester:

she would halt with a scattering of gravel in the station yard at Mount Kisco, just as the commuters' train drew in and her husband stepped to the platform. She would kiss him (but what would be the quality of that kiss—affection?—pity?—remorse? She would kiss him, and) they would drive off home together.

And then the door that was like the doors in all the other bungalows but the door that made them different: the door would close behind them; and all the thousand intimacies, irrelevant but binding, that their life together had imposed on them—these would surround them and bring their weight to bear on them.

The dinner plates and the silver with their remembered patterns, the coffee urn with its handle that was so usual to her touch, the napkins folded as they had been folded after last night's meal, and the chairs in the living room posed as if to continue last night's conversations. And then, the long evening ended, the brushings of the teeth as always as always, and the slipping off of suspenders and the unfastening of garters and the rubbing on and the rubbing off again of the cold cream that would carry away at last all traces of the kisses that had been so sweet in the afternoon. And the slippers in their familiar place and the night gown on its usual hook and the light switch just where the knowing finger reached to press it and then the bungalow sleeping at last in its row of bungalows and they two in their bed together.

It was not that he was jealous. It was just that, no matter what happened, he would never know, and it saddened him. It was just that each time she left him it seemed as if it were forever and in a sense it was forever, for it would be a different Laura who sat at the table under her husband's eye, and it would be a Laura subtly different still—a Laura ever so slightly changed by this other life of hers that he could never know but whose effects he could observe upon her—who would appear next time she drove down to see him.

And the pillows plumped out again when the cleaning woman came tomorrow, and the ash trays emptied, the highball glasses washed and put away as her voice must some day be put away among the silences of the years: it was just that there was so little of her that was his own, and that little so uncompletely captured, so tenuously retained.

I remember that he turned to me suddenly, and his eyes pale with sadness: "What do you do when you make a mistake?" he said. "You can't go back, you know.

"You can only do one thing at a time," he said. "But it's worse than that. Because each thing you do, each step you take, cuts you off forever from all the other steps you might have taken. The other things you might, at that moment, have done.

"We are always advancing," he said. "The only thing you wonder about is, where."

I felt sorry for him, sitting there. I knew so well what he was thinking. For it hardly mattered now at what time his mistake had been made, whether it had been in marrying Helen or in leaving her, in beginning his affair with Laura or at any other point along the twisted course his life had run. In any case, there had been a halt, and a change in direction—or, still more, an attempt to go back and start all over again—that seemed to nullify all that had been gained before. And I knew that now, in the round revealing moment, he sat staring, faced with futility, bound about by despair. "Ah, God!" (I knew) he was thinking. "Why am I here, and how did I come this way?"

I felt, above all, a sense of loss: that he had been lost not only to me but to himself as well in this halt, this change, this belated attempt to return. That he had been lost though Helen might (as most of us who knew them then believed she would) decide in the end to return to him. Lost though he let her go and continued his affair with Laura. Lost though she in her turn divorced her husband and married him, and lost in any other outcome that might ensue.

He was a young man, like any other young man in the city. He was handsome, at that time, and prosperous; his coat sat well on his shoulders, his trousers hung neatly down his legs: you yourself may have passed him, unrecognized and unrecognizing, along the city's streets.

But I, who had known him and recognized him— I never saw him again.

An Instant of Ecstasy

He never knew how it had begun: perhaps it had been that night when (they had all made up a party to go to the Savoy and, dancing and (thuddingly the music: its prompt beat. Its hungering rhythm: conjuringly the lights but the dark faces spattered with laughter and) they two among them but forgetting them. They two in a winged whirling, and) he had been as if enthralled by the mellow union of their bodies, dancing together. The swift unleashing of his ardor. . . .

Or perhaps that afternoon when they had all driven out to the country for a picnic and (he had been watching: as if bringing a sharper tang to the air her clear cool smile, and) she like Autumn's maiden: she running lightly toward him across the grass, and the thin skirt frolicking about her knees. . . . Or once when after the cocktail party and (they were all crowded together under the brownstone stoop waiting for the speakeasy door to open and (he, but hardly daring. But as if carelessly) he had slipped

his arm around her waist and) gently: her hip leaning into his.

But just then the proprietor had come peering and
("Bon jour, Monsieur 'Enderson!") hastily unlatch-
ing the door. . . . Or perhaps even (he never knew)
that time when he had gone out to the kitchen with
her to help mix the drinks, and she kneeling before
the refrigerator tugging at the ice-trays, and (like
an enchantment: he watching) the curve of her arm
from the armpit, and the soft parabolas of her breasts
floating forward under the light stuff of her gown as
she leaning: these had seemed the visible mold of his
desire.

Then her eyes had caught his and for a moment
(while in the living room the others all laughing all
talking, but as if far away and: in the white kitchen
coolness they two alone together and her eyes meeting
his. But he never knew) an invitation trembled in
them. He had made no move, on that night or on any
other. He had not hunted her. He had not even tried
to kiss her. He had been discreet. . . .

It had been a long time, and (there had been these
moments but he hardly (knowing he never) daring.

But he (or as if not himself but: something within him, waiting) watching but) then at last there came the moment that he knew was his.

It was the hour of twilight, and though the room was between them and the room in half-darkness and she (musingly, her fingers arrested on the keys but (proudly the last strong chord, its summons dying sonorously. Over the dark-dreaming surface of the sound) her voice coming lightly distantly. "I haven't played in years," she was saying. "I'm never allowed to play at home. I think it's wonderful your having a piano here," she was saying as (flickeringly the shadows, and) she sitting demurely) talking, and he watching but hardly seeing but he knew.

He knew by the slurred softness of her words as if inattentively dropping and by the new fullness that enriched her lips; by the (tenderly the white throat leaning, and defenselessly over the (oh! vulnerable) breasts. He knew the) warm surrenderingness of her attitude but it was by more than this: it was by the very aroma of desire that now (throbbingly, and like a heaviness on the air. They (in the darkening room as (thicklier the shadows fast falling, and) her voice

211

ceasing. Silence encircled them: they) together breathing, and) like a perfume that wind or distance could not dissipate, and (willingly) her willingness enveloping him. And she (but hastily: "It must sound awful," she) was saying, but as if in his very nostrils, prickingly, he knew.

He waited still, for a moment, but it was a moment that had become tremendous. It was as if all the scattered fragments of their intimacies, at last (combining: gently, the remembered pressure of her hip, and (the light whitely on her arm: she kneeling, and) the gracious swaying of her back against his (guiding, his) hand: as if all those lost moments again claiming him, and) flowing together: combining to build the very body of his passion, articulate and attainable, before him. Across the silent room, she (willingly) waiting.

Her fingers had fallen from the keys. . . .

He found himself standing over her. "Can I make you another drink?" he was saying, but his mouth unwieldy and she half-turning on the piano bench: she slowly lifting her (shining as if shiveringly, her) eyes meeting his and (slowly) shaking her head and:

suddenly, he was on his knees before her, and his arm penning her thighs and his arm circling her waist: his arms weighting her, holding her.

"I must. I must," he was saying helplessly, while her hand like a pent sigh released going straying through his hair. "I must. I must." Then, and: gently, inquiringly. . . .

"No, no. No, no, no," but as if soothingly.

"But I must. I love you."

But no answer, but her lips broodingly brushing his; and then parting, soft and compliant, as his lips rushed to seize hers again. . . .

Her dress was gray, and she wore no underslip, but only (and he fumblingly: he (and his eyes cameras. He) eagerly and, as if dissolving, the sheath of satin and beneath it only the stockings smoke-blue and mistily clouding: moonlike the rising whiteness of her thighs. And he) and then only the lace-crinkled triangle enclosing her hips and, dimly the darker triangle it cradled. Then only the narrow brassière and: her breasts like eyes through a pair of sun-spectacles, peering out with an air at once studious and shy.

"But it's wonderful!" he cried softly, watching her. "Everything about you! Everything you do!"

She turned to him, smiling containedly, and there was a moment when he (seeing the often-seen face above the (till now unknown and hardly guessed at: startlingly, the) bright nudity. For a moment he) felt a bridegroom shyness: as if he hardly dared.

"Silly!" she said.

"Why am I silly?"

"Saying that. When you know it isn't true."

But there is a wonder in a woman's body. One can stare at it forever, and still not see its grace entire: not seize completely the graceful flexing of the ankle as (foamlike: delicately) the last fleck of lace is discarded and (ineffably, the clean curve of the calf slenderly swelling to (here again the sea's touch and the sea's flavor as) shell-like the murmurous hollow behind the knee, and) the knee lifting, displaying the smooth beveling of the flanks: the cool promise of the thighs.

One can stare forever and still not fully, not surroundingly see the hips set in sumptuous symmetry and (where the flesh clothed all in languor but (blithely, the little fluted fold, and) graciously receiving. The hips clenching, relaxing and (now knee locked to knee, and thighs in fervent union as) searchingly, but all merging, tumbling. All slowly revolving, and) her back like a slim whip swaying. Liquidly, her breasts yielding softly under his pressure.

And the clamped shoulders, the prisoning arms. The teeth that can do such tender damage and the lips that can assuage it: the lips (gropingly, through the tangle of kisses impeding her (no o no) but gaspingly, and: her eyes closing. And he lifting her head from the pillow, and: the tossed hair streaming as (no o no no o) but deliciously as: her eyes flaring opening and) furiously seeking: her lips as (o now no o now now) and, but dyingly. But only tremblingly: the last faint internal shivers and softly, her lips parting again to accept his, but as if freshly, dewily. . . .

Outside the window, the world had grown suddenly dark.

Sunday Morning on Fifth Avenue

"Harootunian," she said. "It *is* a funny name."

"Haven't you ever noticed it? It's a big store, really, up at the corner of Twenty-second Street, and they have the most marvellous rugs in the windows."

They two, and these others by twos: all (in the bright clean intimate air slowly strolling and (before them the wide avenue slicing the heart of the gleaming city (before them: welcomingly the towers shaved thin by the sunlight) slanting before them to the immediate immensity of the sky, but) here the street lying still half-shadowed and (half-sleeping: still, here) only the upper windows waking blinking but the sidewalks cool and spacious, and only they two and these too: scatteredly, the straying couples) pleasantly promenading, their friendly heel-taps lightly sprinkling the Sunday morning (still) serenity. Across the street, the sun was tickling the grass in the First Presbyterian churchyard. Each apartment house awning offered a benediction as they passed. He took her arm.

"You look lovely. And you look so pure, too."

"Pure?"

"I never saw anyone look so pure. It must be that gray dress. You look lovely in it."

Until then not turning, but now: deliberately, and her eyes under the stiff little brim of her hat aimed incitingly up into his.

"You think purity becomes me?"

"You know what I think about that."

And: feeling her arm squeezing his hand softly against the (secretly) softness of her body. Suddenly there shot through him a (moment, a) memory of the night and that (memory, pricking a) moment when, but (and their tumbled breathing: when (insistently, the night (as if limitlessly, and the melting whiteness of her body: when, she leaning (above him her (muffling, her) hair and, cloudily) her lost smile in the pink-crinkled darkness when) and cramming them together. It had been a moment when both spent and lying loosely: when fondlingly among the complacent senses. Then, and) his hands holding her slim waist like a vase that one lifts to drink from: his hands claimingly on the soft flesh, and then (swooping to envelop him. He remembered that softness, and) remembering her embracing smile. And then: but NOW, and) they were walking and it seemed as if he could not withdraw his eyes from hers.

"You're sweet," she said. "But you mustn't hold my arm like that. People will think we're husband and wife, out for a stroll."

"Well, aren't we? Almost?"

And (but a bus going grumblingly past, and (up where in front of the Longchamps at Twelfth Street a little cluster of ladies skinnily signalling: the bus) halting, and the ladies awkwardly, one by one. But he, and) now strangely, her slow unaccepting gaze.

"I suppose so," she said. "Almost. . . ."

And, like a shadow between them but (the ladies clinging precariously to the stair rail, as) with a blatting of its exhaust, the bus starting off again: closing the incident. It (perhaps?) was (the incident?) going (trailing?) to RIVERSIDE DRIVE 5TH AVE —57 ST.

Or perhaps if they had spoken: if (when the man pacing out from Thirteenth Street: the man (solemnly, when he reached the corner, turning and (like a sentry, gravely turning) and: going pacing back again. And) they both watching separately, but with deep attention. "Almost," she had said and then silence settling between them: a silence that (swelling uncomfortably, like a bubble in the ear but) hardening between them. If he had found the word to say, or if she) turning laughing, sharingly when (they two: like any other two walking but now silently, and) maybe at Korn's Klock Korner but: "Almost," he had said and: but if even at Fourteenth Street they had turned back.

But (but a bright blue roadster, pressing triumphantly onward) they crossed and (they walking: like a door of stone slowly shutting) the buildings closing behind them. The buildings (and a solemn chill of emptiness flowing out from the (blankly, the) shop windows) as if frozen solid. They walking and: damp and deep-shadowed, the hewn avenue. "Almost," he had said, and now it was too late.

Let this be our chamber, then, this endless avenue: this pavement our couch and this stony firmament our sky, wide and starry with:

I. Freedman & Co. WIENER & KATZ

R
E
I
S
E
R

BROS.

RAU
FASTENER
CO.

ACME
PANTS
CO.

MAX GAMSA, Inc.
"GAYTOWN" CLOTHES

HERO SHIRT

Jos. J. Siegel
STOUTS and SLIMS

ROTARY
SHIRT

"GROTTAMAID" NECKWEAR

M   E   R   O   D   E

Let BAYUK CIGARS be our flaming sun.

Let LUNA HOSIERY shed its brooding light upon us.

Let THE HOME OF PUSSYWILLOW CHOCOLATES be our home too.

Let ANNIN & CO unfurl their banners above us as we go marching, bearing our bitterness proudly unrelentingly past the (grim-walled, the) METH-ODIST BOOK CONCERN. But let us not (even as if (so lightly: if) just accidentally?) touch each

220

other's hand. Let us not (even momentarily?) meet the other's (quickly: each glancing) eyes.

"Here we are," he (at last, he) said.

And there before them the deep red, the abiding purple: tumbling, the autumnal yellows over the shadowed green, and the angular blossoms tangled intricately. Like a faraway landscape lit by ancient suns, the great rug revealed itself, calm and resplendent, in the window at Harootunian's. They stood staring.

"I would marry you, you know," he said. "You ought to know that."

"I know."

Darkly green, like a lawn at twilight, and the flowers incredibly violet, endlessly intertwined. The rug was draped in soft folds and the folds rose gently, forming a tiny hillock on whose top the templed gods might play. The texture smooth as moss, and as if moistly shining.

"Well, why not, then? Why not just go ahead and do it?"

"I don't know, darling. Really I don't."

"You must have some reason."

"Does one have to have a reason for everything?"

Palely, the yellow, and the angular blossoms tracing the tangle of the vines. The crimson dripping quietly among the leaves. Like a faraway landscape, lit by ancient suns, the rug rose calm and resplendent before them. She projected her laugh toward it, a bitterness for them to traverse.

"What a mess!" she said. "And anyway, how do we know it would work?"

"Why wouldn't it work? Good Lord! Don't we love each other?"

"I know. But maybe this isn't the kind of thing that lasts."

"Oh, but you know it would. I know it would, anyway. And so do you. Now, don't you?"

"I suppose so. Yes."

"Well, why not, then? We don't want to go on like this forever, do we? Wasting both our lives?"

Moss-moist and unbelievably verdant: darkly the green, like a lawn at twilight, and the flowers endlessly intertwined. Tumbling, the yellows: the crimson dripping quietly among the leaves.

As if at a faraway landscape they stood staring, both knowing that on such fields as these their feet would never tread.

A Gesture in Conclusion

And there was that night when (but coming into
the room almost furtively, switching on the lights
glancing quickly about, as if he feared it might har-
bor some surprise for him. All was as (always: as)
always the furniture the green-tinted atmosphere
of the room passively accepting him as he (and yet
disturbingly, the sense of something portentous, something strange: as) he moved forward slowly. The
piano gleamed satiny, eying him with a sidewise ex-
pectant glance like a colt fresh-released from the
stable; volubly the brown armchair and the small
table rubbing purring against its stolid legs: the
books on the shelves (as he, passing) watching
solemn silent attentive as sidewalk watchers of a fu-
neral procession and (there the three rush-bottom
chairs turning their backs to him in mysterious col-
loquy: the (cluttered, the) marble mantel-piece. It's
as if something more were to come, he thought. It's as
if someone else were expected, he thought, as) the

224

mirror staring through and beyond him, frankly interested only in the opposite wall. He standing staring, and) suddenly, he knew the way it would end.

Or rather, the many ways but, suddenly (realizingly: it was all as if months had passed. The weary months that (even now) he dreaded facing and he (uncertainly. But it would be morning. He would be making his coffee over the little electric grill. It would have come to that: to the bagfull of biscuits brought home from the baker's every evening, to the eggs in their cardboard carton and the small jar of cream economically preserved. He would be making his lonely morning coffee and) but almost unbelievingly, hearing the locked door opening: hearing the entering step! And) turning, and: "Helen!" his glad cry ringing.

She would be standing, small, shy, timidly appealing, before him. And her traveling bag dropped at her feet as if all defenses abandoned and (but touchingly: as if clutching the last shreds of her self-possession, she) but breathlessly, saying: "Isn't it lucky I kept my key?

"As soon as I found I had my key I knew I'd have

to surprise you," she would be saying, but only just to be keeping talking. "So I didn't write you or cable you or anything. As soon as I found it I just—," and then breakingly: "Dearest, do you really want me back?"

And he (but, and sweeping: as if all of her into his arms) and: "Helen! You know I do."

And she happily, through the excited tears: "Because I just had to come. Somehow. I just *had* to."

But he, with no words, but (only: tenderly the first few kisses and then more fiercely. But) she suddenly, remembering: "Dearest, there's a taxi downstairs. We mustn't keep it waiting."

But he only: "Let it wait."

To begin all over again, he thought. To go back, and forget the way we came. Or rather, the many ways but (as if now in his ears: hearing the downstairs bell ringing startlingly. And then clicking the clicker and (already a nameless apprehension wormlike stirring, as he: listening, and) the unfamiliar yet strangely familiar step coming up the stair. He in the doorway waiting defenseless, as) rising to confront him: the figure that embodied all his accusations. The figure charged with doom.

And what then? What then, as he (while already the cold sweat starting: he (wildly: "Why, hello there, old man. Why, hello there. What brings you down around here at this time of night?" With a fearful glibness, he) feverishly: "But come in, old man. Come in and sit down. Well, it's good to see you. Sit over there." He, fawningly) spreading the words like his cloak of pride for the other to walk on, as the man entering, ignoring his outstretched hand? And then bluntly, grimly: "I made up my mind I'd come down and see you. About my wife."

And then the protests, the exclamations of false surprise and the trembling assurances as (he swiftly scatteredly: he spinning the cowardly screen of words but the other's eye coldly piercing. He exclaiming, protesting, but) the other watching unheeding, as if behind the sweating words he heard some calmer, more momentous adjuration.

And then he pausing as if he too had heard the voice of doom.

And then, and before he could even blink his eyes

against the shattering whiteness suddenly enveloping
him: the bursting blast of the pistol shot.

"I told you I'd made up my mind."

Or rather, the many ways but (now all fleetingly:
or as if the months that would have passed, but their
passing no longer mattered. Or the tears that would
have been shed, or the quarrels begun or the recon-
ciliations effected. Or the lips crushed mournfully
against the highball glass, the eyes looking pleadingly
into his, or the destroying rages or the precarious
renewals: all in the long slow twisting drawing-out of
passion to its slender end but (now all running together. Now in the silent night as (if Time (silently)
collapsing all around him. Restlessly, his hands moving among the clutter on the mantel-piece, and) his
hands picking up the dull bronze dancing figure.
Hers, he thought, but) only fleetingly. And then
setting it down and: as if the act had acquired a final
significance. I know so well how it will end, he thought.
I've been through it all already. And like the only
sound in the world (through the window: reminding
him) a motor car, its tires chuckling rubberly, passing in the street below. And) then his eye meeting the

eye of his image in the mirror and he for a moment staring. As a gaunt castaway might stare with dulled eyes into the mirror he staring, seeing himself as the pitiful survivor after shipwreck and disaster.

And then (perhaps) slowly striding to the open window and looking down at the converging lines of the building beneath him, at the whole swift falling-away of the façade; and then (slowly, confidently) leaning out against the breast of Fate: and the long rush downward.

Then, perhaps, the telephone ringing, ringing unanswered.

Then, perhaps, the knocking at the door.

I passed soon after.

TOPIC SENTENCES, IV.

Tonight I Will Follow Strangers

Tonight I Will Follow Strangers . . .

Often, it seems I have no friends—or rather, I have friends, but all of them have Watkins, Algonquin or Stuyvesant telephone numbers and live in the Village. Tonight, I will have none of them: I know so well what they are doing. Moreover, to see them I must first arrange the meeting over the telephone: I know too the disappointment, the chagrin that can follow on the use of that instrument.

Who has not known humiliation, self-abasement, as he waited in the coin-box booth like a man spying from his hiding place on an emissary parleying for him: listening sullen and impatient while it rang and paused, rang and paused, rang again and at last stood mute before him, as if lacking even the words to say, "Go. You are not wanted here"?

Who, having tried one number and had no answer, has not rung up friend after friend, merely to reassure himself that some one of them will reply; and, none answering, has not pulled out his pocket address book and called still others—some of them perhaps persons whom he has neglected, has not seen in months, so that to speak with them now would be an embarrassment—and meanwhile jiggling the hook, exhorting the operator, insisting that they *must* answer and receiving with dismay her reiteration that they do not: who has not, finally, felt uncertainties, self-questionings (do they refuse to answer because they divine that it is I who calls? Must I always hammer, hammer on their doors until from very weariness they admit me? Belabor them with importunities until grudgingly they reply?) and ended by slinking from the drug store, to roam the streets in bitter loneliness?

Shall I ever forget that night on Lexington Avenue, on one of my visits to the city last autumn?

The irony of the situation was heightened by the fact that I had just left a friend's apartment, where I had had cocktails and had refused a dinner invitation on the ground of a previous engagement. I had, as a matter of fact, no engagement.

Instead, that night, I had told myself I would follow strangers. I would go alone to Ninety-sixth Street

and Broadway; I would dine (with a tabloid newspaper propped against the paper napkin container
before me, and a vigilant and observant eye for the
behavior of the Jewish families sitting eating in noisy
contentment around me) in one of those delicatessen
restaurants of the neighborhood, all marble and mir-
rors and amber lights.

Later, I would spend the evening wandering on the
teeming sidewalks and (enjoying the tumult, the glitter: the light from shop-windows rippling over
faces passing, the bus-tops looming like illuminated
balloons, the voices in conversations caught over my
shoulder that I alone would have leisure to listen to,
the gestures that I alone would observe. I was walking up Lexington Avenue, with light dripping drop
by drop from the Chrysler Building and the lanterne
of the New York Central tower coming up like a
nocturnal sun over the houses across the street, but
already seeing myself up Broadway slowly strolling
and slowly down again: not lonely but isolated—a being stripped of self, nameless and voiceless but with
vigilant observant eye) threading the crowds hurrying to Loew's Riverside, to Healey's Sunken Gardens,
to the Whelan's on the corner for a double-rich malted

milk with whipped cream and an egg salad sandwich.
Finally, I would go over to Riverside Drive and (accompanied on my right by the river, pleasantly, gently, silently flowing) I would walk down to Seventy-second Street and so on to my hotel and to bed.

I was walking up Lexington Avenue when suddenly it occurred to me that it was as yet only a little past six o'clock: why not find someone to have a drink with me in the hour before my expedition started?

I entered the drug store at the corner, made my way to the telephone booth at the end of the soda fountain, and called Circle-7 6653. Awkwardly, with one hand I managed to extract a cigarette from the pack in my pocket and lighted it, listening to the rhythmic buzzing, buzzing which tallied and even seemed muffledly to echo the ringing, ringing in my friend's apartment.

There was no answer.

And then the fever took me. I rang up friend after friend and, these not answering, I pulled out my pocket address book and called still others. I jiggled the hook. I exhorted the operator.

Note, however, that my original plan was as yet

unchanged. I still intended to go to Ninety-sixth Street and Broadway for an evening alone, but now it seemed that first I must speak to someone, if only to bid him good-bye. I must reassure myself that the excursion would be a voluntary one, and not an exile.

But soon I had capitulated even in this, and I was calling others whose habits or whose plans I knew with certainty—who would be drinking cocktails till eight o'clock or later, then crowding together into taxicabs, wildly riding to this restaurant or that (I would go with them)—who would turn on the radio and insist on dancing (I would dance with them)— who would have arranged an evening of bridge (I would sit on the sofa drinking my solitary drink and looking up brightly whenever at the end of a hand someone addressed a remark to me). I would do anything, go anywhere, to escape being condemned to spend an evening alone in the city.

The operator: "They do not answer."
Myself: "But they *must* answer."
The operator: "I will ring them again."

And now came uncertainties, self-questionings.

Worse: at this moment glancing out through the window in the door of the booth, I met the eye of the soda fountain clerk. He was observing me with a curious interest. Near him, at the counter, a man whom I took to be the proprietor of the store was standing chatting with two friends, a man and a woman: all were regarding me with a gaze at once attentive and amused.

I blush now to describe my subsequent procedure, but at the moment it seemed the only course to follow. Calling one more number, and hardly waiting for the fateful unanswered buzzing to sound in my ears, I launched on an elaborate mimicry of a telephonic conversation. I laughed, I gesticulated; while the mouthpiece of the instrument reared back haughty and amazed I talked gaily and animatedly into the nothingness it represented. Finally, as if impatient to join a group of charming friends who already with equal impatience awaited me, I pulled the door of the booth half open, still talking brightly.

"Oh, I'll be down in about a quarter of an hour, Joe," I said.

"Sure, Joe," I said. "Want me to bring anything in?"

(At this moment the operator cut in, saying, "Stuyvesant-9 1262 does not answer. Shall I ring them again?")

"O.K., Joe," I replied. "I'll be right down."

What her next remark may have been I cannot guess. I hung up and, issuing from the booth, demanded of the soda fountain clerk two bottles of ginger ale.

"Large bottles," I specified. "Pale dry."

He dropped them deftly into a paper bag. I took my purchase under my arm and, assuming a festive anticipatory smile, strode out into the street—even, I recall, pausing outside the door (but in view of those inside) to scan the street as if to hail a taxicab, before I moved on up Lexington Avenue, with bitter loneliness as my prospect for the evening.

Never to knuckle under: that is the lesson of the city. Walk its wastes as you would a wilderness, unconscious of the myriad eyes upon you. For let the explorer once give heed to the impression that here, pendulous on that viny branch, a python hangs waiting—that there a jaguar crouches in the underbrush or beyond, among the rocks, a party of savages lies concealed: that everywhere, hostile eyes are watching him—and his doom is sealed. The same studied inattentiveness is needed, if you would traverse Times Square and not go mad.

I have been too conscious of their eyes. Let me confess it: I can hardly reach the limit of the most casual stroll and turn back along the way I have come without trying to justify my action to whoever may be observing me. I snatch out my watch, glance at it, turn back hastily; or I peer at the house numbers, mumble my lips as if repeating an address, walk back with an air of retracing my steps; or I look up puzzled, like one who in pursuit of his thoughts has been led out of his way.

So—to the woman standing in the tenement entrance, to the grocer's boy piling empty crates along the curb, to the iceman whose head just rises from his cellar-way—I explain my reversal of routes: I am a man who has suddenly remembered an important engagement; or one who, on an errand, has been led past his destination; or one who has merely wandered slightly astray, contemplating the intricacies of his business affairs.

Or like the explorer: though conscious of their ob-

240

servant eyes, consider that it may be timidity that
makes them watchful. They will not attack you, unless startled; therefore, make your actions understandable within their reasoning. If you must wander, do so
with an air of purpose—to the denizens of these industrious thoroughfares, aimlessness is incomprehen-
sible. Turn back like one recalled by an important
engagement, start down side streets as if an errand
led you most imperatively in that direction. Above
all, never knuckle under.

Or, at worst, choose one among them and follow
him, letting his course, his actions, determine yours.
Never let them follow you: for then they gain confidence, and become dangerous.

But I have not told all that occurred on that night
last autumn. Naturally, I did not go to Ninety-sixth
Street and Broadway. Instead, I roamed the streets—
up Lexington Avenue to Forty-seventh Street and so
across to Broadway—thence northward to Columbus
Circle—down Fifty-ninth Street—north again on
Ninth Avenue. Having no destination before me, it
was hard to escape the impression that my impulsion
came from the rear. Who flees, but one pursued?

Often, I would pause before some shop window, to study with an air of rapt attention the objects on display there. After a sufficient number of those who had been following me had passed the spot where I had posted myself, I would again take up the march—now, however, following *them*. It is easy to remain in command of a situation, if one brings his intelligence to bear on it.

Or another expedient: I would stop short, cock an ear as if my name had been called, look questingly about and then, with an eager wave of the hand, dart across the street to the opposite sidewalk.

But again, there were times when in spite of my precautions I would feel all my self draining out of me. Wandering aimless, nameless where no one knew me and having not even the voice to cry my name, so brushed against and buffeted that the integument within which my character, my purpose and my person live incorporate had been scoured away, I would become as if ghostly: a creature disembodied and unreal, from whom all emotions and all actions human or inhuman are expectable—down some dim avenue another nocturnal figure slipping furtive and anonymous among the dark shops, the silent houses, and indistinguishable from any other one might encounter, hurrying no one knows whither down the empty street. You may have seen me and wondered: often, passing a stranger, I saw as it were my own glance reflected in his eyes, and read my own bewilderment and dismay on his countenance.

That was a night of horror, and yet I have not confessed the whole of the episode. You will remember that I described how, prisoned in the telephone booth, I was embarrassed by the presence of the proprietor of the drug store and his friends, maliciously observing my discomfiture; and how, half-opening the door that they might hear, I mimicked conversation with a friend at the other end of the wire. But I have not told that, emerging from the booth, I could not resist a temptation to address them.

In shipwreck, in accident, in all times when stress of excitement or of danger overcomes the normal reticences, strangers will accept an intimacy with one another that they might otherwise reject, and surely at that moment my emotions had reached an almost catastrophic intensity. So, as I passed these three, I paused. "That was Joe," I told them. "He wants me to come right down."

They made no reply. They sat as if amazed—or as if abashed, scenting in my remark an implied reprimand for having spied on me—or perhaps as if merely envious, grudging me what pleasures the evening might hold in store for me. I could not read their expressions. Their eyes met mine flatly; their faces were fixed and frozen like those of persons surprised by a flashlight photograph, where the grimace records, not the response to the picture itself, but the emotions of the instant anterior to it. It is so that I see their faces now: like the faces of persons seen in a flashlight photograph. It was because of them that I bought the ginger ale.

Nor have I told how I disposed of those two bottles. I carried them as far as Lexington Avenue and Forty-seventh Street: there, I overtook an elderly gentleman strolling slowly. I matched my steps to his just long enough to accustom him to my presence at his side, yet not long enough to render him uneasy. Then: "D'you mind holding this till I tie my shoe?" I said, very casually, and handed him the bag containing the bottles. He took it, of course. I ran.

But mark the subtlety of my stratagem. Experience in the city has taught me a certain craft in such matters. Had I dealt with him as man to man, told him frankly my predicament, explained that in offering him the ginger ale I was merely seeking to disembarrass myself of a commodity for which I had no use whatever—he would instantly have become frightened, suspicious, resentful.

I approached him differently. Look at it this way, I put it to him tacitly: here are two men, walking together up Lexington Avenue of an evening. One, who happens to be carrying a parcel, discovers that his shoelace is untied. What more natural, then, than that he should hand over the encumbrance to his companion, asking him to hold it for a moment that both his hands may be free to manipulate the knot?

Thus, with slyness I managed to make the whole affair seem simple, reasonable, natural. Accepting the matter in that light, and therefore receiving without demur the parcel from my hands, the elderly gentleman I speak of overlooked one important objection to my argument: that we were not acquainted with each other. When this occurred to him, it was too late.

It will be seen, then, that delicacy is needed. Before the wild beast from the jungle can be brought to accept man as his master, the trainer must first induce in the animal a feeling of confidence in him. By a thousand delicate stratagems, he sets himself patiently to demonstrate that his presence in the cage is not dangerous or ominous. Once the animal is convinced of this, the trainer may with ease teach it to do his bidding.

But mark: though I have said that the man is the master of the animal, he is not such. On the contrary, the whole course of his relationship to it is a process of subjecting himself to it, of governing himself according to its modes of conduct, of suiting his actions to its way of thinking. The lion tamer, entering the cage, must do as the lion would have him do: his least departure from the routine of the performance is met with the teeth, the claws, the pandemoniac fury of the beast.

So with these others. Never frighten or outrage them. Be delicate; equal yourself to them; see that nothing you do shall pass beyond the limits of their comprehension. Are you moved to address the man seated opposite you in the Child's Restaurant? Descending from the Elevated station to the bright street below, do you feel impelled to begin a conversation with the young lady moving step by step beside you like your partner accompanying you down the grand staircase to a ball room? Beware of elaborate tentatives, of timid avowals: these will only perplex them and arouse their suspicions. Limit yourself instead rigidly to the commonplace. Invest the transaction with the aura of the usual. Say to him casually, "Your necktie is crooked."

Say to her with a friendly interest, "Which way do you go from here, east or west?" His hand will go to his collar; she will answer you. In either case, it will be but an instant before your companion realizes that your assumption of friendship rests on no basis whatsoever. But, meantime, you will have enjoyed a moment of true intimacy with them—an intimacy the purer because it can not last. This has its value, to the lonely wanderer.

Or again: there come moments when one seems to recognize a friend in every passer-by. I can not tell the cause of it, nor can I specify whether the effect is predominantly pleasing or disturbing, but have you never had the experience: that each oncomer approaching wears the lineaments of some old and nearly forgotten friend, that the passing crowd becomes suddenly a parade of long-dead recollections—you discerning everywhere in it the faces of schoolmates, boyhood companions, vanished acquaintances whose very names you have forgotten—you staring bewilderedly while, unnoticing and unconcerned, they pass? How has the occurrence affected you? How have you explained it?

Shall I ever forget that night last autumn? There were adventures that will not bear thinking of, episodes that I hesitate to relate. I have not told all. Leaving the drug store, I roamed the streets: leaving it as one would leave a judgment room, where he had called on all his friends to aid him and had had none answer; roaming the streets as such a one would, after the betrayal. You may have seen me, and wondered: often, passing a stranger, I saw as it were my own glance reflected in his eyes, and read my own bewilderment and dismay on his countenance.

I peered at house numbers, mumbling my lips as if repeating an address, turned back to retrace my steps with an air of one who has been led out of his way. Cocking an ear, then waving an eagerly welcoming hand, I circumvented them by darting suddenly across

248

the street to the opposite sidewalk. Passing a Chock Full O' Nuts shop I encountered a girl, just issuing from the door. She wore a tight gray coat; her face was plump and petulant; her eyes, round and blue, were intriguingly magnified by thick-lensed nose glasses. Altogether, a remarkably attractive creature.

I seized her hand, bowed, and smiled. While she stared wonderingly, I bowed again. "Sorry," I said. "But I must be going. Call me up some time, won't you?" And hurried on. It had been a pleasant meeting.

Or: snatching out my watch, glancing at it, turning back hastily; or the top-hatted man, white-mufflered, pacing down Madison Avenue, halting at my tap on his shoulder; or the woman turning sharply down Seventy-eighth Street from Columbus Avenue, and her white face glancing back at me slouching, hands in pockets, after her: I made my actions understandable within their reasoning.

Or: the little crowd (I passing: the crowd) clotted at the curbing, hungrily staring. On the anvil pavement the crushed and bleeding body, the limbs dreadfully awry, the wide eyes empty and from the staved-in chest one last moan escaping—the body smashed by the hammer blows of height, and (I passing, and) the crowd: hungrily staring.

It is so that I see their faces now—like the faces of persons seen in a flashlight photograph.

And always the pavement stretching infinitely before me, the limitless assemblage of houses: the sudden gushings of light from shop windows, the mysterious illuminations behind drawn curtains: my heels gripped as if in steel and as if strings quivering down the backs of my legs, my feet soddenly in my shoes: dim lights down side streets, glowing snowily. But there were times when I became as if ghostly, a creature disembodied and unreal, from whom all emotions and all actions human or inhuman are expectable—down some dim avenue another nocturnal figure slipping furtive and anonymous among the dark shops, the silent houses, and indistinguishable from any other one might encounter hurrying no one knows whither down the empty street.

Toward midnight I found myself before the apartment house in which Henderson had lived when last I knew him. Acting on a sudden impulse, I entered the vestibule, inspected the names listed on the letter boxes there. His was among them. I rang his bell.

There was a pause, and then the apparatus for releasing the door lock began clicking. The sound had an odd effect on me: it made me realize, suddenly, how defenseless he was. Somewhere in the recesses of the building above he stood in a room, pushing a button, and how did he know whom or what—robber, murderer, madman, avenger—he might thus be admitting to his presence? As much for my own protection as for his (for how did I know in what mood, having these to choose from, I might mount the stairs?) I hurried from the building into the street again.

"Better telephone first," I told myself. "Make sure that I'm not disturbing him."

Leaving the building, I knew I would not telephone him. Passing the drug store at the corner, I knew I would. I entered, made my way to the telephone booth at the end of the soda fountain, called his number.

There was no answer.

Myself: "But they *must* answer."
The operator: "I will ring them again."

And again I heard the rhythmic buzzing, buzzing which tallied and even seemed muffledly to echo the ringing, ringing in my friend's apartment—the telephone ringing, ringing unanswered.

But now I could listen no longer. Fear, of I knew not what tragic eventuality—fear had gripped me. I jammed the receiver down on its hook, yanked open the door of the telephone booth. I went hurrying back down the street to his apartment house. I went racing up his stairs.

A moment more, and my noisy fist was hammering on the panels of his door. I, in the yellow hallway, frantic and breathless, my brain dizzy and reeling beneath the blind cudgelings of fear: I hammering, but from the room within (where (I knew, the (as always, the) furniture, passively the green-tinted atmosphere and the piano, gleaming satiny: cluttered, the marble mantel-piece and) the mirror, frankly interested only in the opposite wall. From the room within) came no answering movement.

From the room within only the terrible silence of catastrophe, the thick unbudging silence boding only doom, and I hammering unavailingly against it: I, knocking on the door.

(And even then, below on the anvil pavement, the

little crowd clotted at the curbing. The crowd: hungrily staring, and I (passing) hastily):

Strangers, do you remember me? You whom I, passing, saw—not only on that night but on many others—and, seeing, vividly remembered: do you remember me? You, pale lovely girl who came riding into the Thirty-fourth Street station like a young queen-elect in her coronation car and (the El train halting and (as if our meeting had been postponed for years but nevertheless inevitably: you and I at last brought face to face and) only the iron gate between. And the gate opening, and) but the crowd drawing back as before a queen, as you descending and I (almost, I) took your hand?

Or you from the bus-top deeply gazing, and that piercing meeting of the eyes: have you, as I have, remembered? Or you on Fourteenth Street that night so long ago, and the quarter spinning flashing in the light of the arc lamp; you on the sidewalk at Pleasantville, with your brief case coming briskly professionally; you, just (delicately: emerging, and) entering the portals of The Tailored Woman; you, little man who (and leading me (but only a block or two, but)

253

so surely, as) hurrying down Forty-second Street;
you, turning the corner at Times Square, or with bent
apologetic shoulders, or that night on the Bowery
when, in the old brown reefer jacket: all you whom the
crowd presented to me as if (meaningfully: the meeting as if) forever, but then in the crowd quickly lost
again—do you remember me?

Or the brushings of arm against arm, the hip swaying gently, the touch of the shoulder, the touch of the
hand—all as if accidentally in the casual pressures of
the crowd, and yet as if even the accident had its meaning in a larger purpose—are these remembered, and
by whom else but me?

Or the window demonstrator patiently tapping the
pane in the drug store window, and then (and his
pointer, like the little bouncing ball in the songs at the
movies dipping gracefully over the (word by word:
"No Pain. No Cutting. No Prying. The Corn Simply
Falls Out. Money Back Guarantee." He spelling patiently, as if for me alone) the printed message. And
then) with such luring gestures: he tapping. "Step
Inside For 25¢ Trial Box." But the crowd (and I
among them) turning coldly ungratefully away.

Or the woman I followed that night down West

Seventy-eighth Street, and (it was wholly accidental. I had no intention, but (and she glancing back: her white face as) I slouching after her. But) she darting fearfully into the apartment house entrance and: hastily jamming the door. And I hurrying onward, as guilty as if I had pursued her with fiendish intentions, into the black hallway.

Or the young man, and his eyes (like a burnt match: gleaming, and my eyes as well) as he following, at Union Square; or the party of merrymakers so gaily crowding into the Subway station, all strangers, all oblivious to me, but I joining them: where are they now, and what has become of them?

Henderson, I know, was somewhere—is somewhere —among them. His life was woven of such incidents as these: its course directed by these casual pressures, and given such meaning as it had for him by these glances, these momentary readings of the eyes. He was a young man, like any other young man in the city: I saw him only occasionally and as if at random, and even then at each meeting it was as if a different Henderson presented himself to me. Even then it was as if the city had come between.

And then, at last, the city surrounded him, made itself a part of him as he of it and (blending together: losing himself as if one by one, and (but even more subtly changing: like a crowd that has not yet compacted itself, but splitting apart, dividing and subdividing. He) as if dispersing, as if lost in very multiplicity, even as I approached. He like a crowd and himself lost in the crowd, and) vanishing, finally, before my eyes.

I never saw him again.

Afterword

By MALCOLM COWLEY

Let me reintroduce you to Robert M. (for Myron) Coates. I first met him in Paris, 1922, and I was his friend, sometimes his neighbor, for more than fifty years. But did I really know him? Open to friendship as he seemed to be, always ready to explain himself, there was in him something inaccessible. It was as if, in his travels through the world, he carried with him a portable, un-windowed room into which he sometimes retired, and locked the door.

Oh, I know the exterior facts about him. Born April 6, 1897, in New Haven, Connecticut. Only child of Frederick and Harriet Davidson Coates. The father, descended from a line of Yankee mechanics, was a tool designer who wandered from New England to the Pacific Northwest and back again, usually as head of his own small enterprise; once he leased a gold mine near Cripple Creek. The boy grew up in more cities than laid claim to Homer; some of them were Springfield (Massachusetts), Portland (Oregon), Seattle, Denver, Cincinnati, Buffalo, and

New York. As a rule he was the lonely new boy in each school he attended, with the result that he was thrown back on his own resources; he read and dreamed. But the family perched longer than usual in Rochester, New York, and there he finished high school after making friends.

Yale, class of '19. Served for some months as a cadet in Naval Aviation, but the Great War ended in time for him to go back to college and graduate with his class. Did publicity work in New York and dropped it to write poetry while living chiefly on lentils. Went to France in 1921 (his father helped) and stayed there for five years. Most of the time he lived above the blacksmith shop in Giverny, a village fifty miles down the Seine from Paris, but he also became a familiar figure in Montparnasse, almost a perambulatory landmark. Very tall, square-shouldered, close to being gaunt in those days when money for meals was a problem, he had a big head (7 ¾) and a solemn oblong face surmounted by a jungle of crinkly red hair through which he couldn't push a comb. His eyes were sky-blue, his cheeks were pink, and, as he slowly bicycled through the Paris streets, people stared at him from sidewalk tables. "He looked like a flag," Janet Flanner said.

He came back to New York in 1926 with two novels, the first of which remained in manuscript. The second was *The Eater of Darkness*, already published in Paris, but in a very limited edition; it combined a scrupulous accuracy of detail with a headlong impossibility of plot.

Republished here in 1929, it has enjoyed an underground reputation as the first, and for some time the only, Dadaist novel in English. Before it appeared, Coates had joined the staff of a very young magazine, *The New Yorker*. There he collaborated on "Talk of the Town," then wrote a weekly book page, then finally—for thirty years—served as art critic. He did his journalistic work in the city, but during most of those years he also had a country house—two houses in succession, both among fields and woods—where he wrote his novels and stories. His avocations were chess, gardening, skiing, and wandering alone in the Manhattan streets.

He published a dozen books, most of them fiction, all of them truly *written*, with an appearance of ease that is among the hardest qualities to master; the question is why he never became as famous as some of his friends and contemporaries. Twice he stood on the front doorstep of fame while we waited to see the door open and hear the band strike up. The first time was in 1930, when he published *The Outlaw Years*, about the land pirates of the Natchez Trace, a book that has been many times reissued. It was chosen by the Literary Guild, but the royalties went into the first of his country houses (that one in Sherman, Connecticut, on a back road to which I moved a few years later). Coates finished the house with his own hands. He says of it in *Yesterday's Burdens*, "I test the floor I laid to see that it does not creak; I inspect the joinings of the door-casings I put in place, the smooth surface of the table I built. These are joys stolen from past centuries. Who nowadays can point to a tree he planted or hang his immortality on a nail of his own driving?" But houses change hands, and Coates's friends concluded that the building of this one had cost him the writing of at least two books for which a public was waiting. His other approach to fame was in 1948, when *Wisteria Cottage,* a novel about a homicidal maniac, almost became a best seller and was almost bought by the movies. But he waited seven years to publish his next novel, *The Farther Shore,* which almost failed to have an audience. It proved to be the last of Coates's longer fictions. He continued, though, to write short stories that should be reread and reissued; perhaps their time will come.

During the last three years of his life he was trying to finish one story—only one—to round out a book that he hoped would be his best collection. But he was wasting away with cancer, and he died February 8, 1973, with the story and the book unfinished.

Those are the facts of his career, and they don't tell us much about the inner man. After fifty years of companionship, and affection too, I still feel that he eludes me. Why, for example, did he reject the notion of trying to become a famous writer? He must have played with the notion more than once, and he must have felt that fame would be gratifying if it came as the unplanned-for result of something he had worked on for years, but he didn't promote his work or trumpet himself. He was more admired by fellow writers and by magazine editors, who printed almost everything he offered them, than he was read by the public at large. He never taught, never went on lecture tours, and never addressed a public meeting, although, in the contentious 1930s, he attended some of these. If he spoke from the floor, it was only to offer a suggestion in a low, diffident voice, as if to apologize for his conspicuous appearance. Why did he prefer to stay in the background? I am sure it was not because of uncertainty about the rightness of his opinions or the value of his work. Perhaps he felt that too much fame would involve him in temptations like those to which some of his early friends had yielded.

A letter of August 8, 1966, was one of the very few in which he allowed himself to complain. He says in part:

> Hemingway—well, he is one of those problems that have always defeated me—like Jim Thurber; the man who gets worse, both as an artist and as a person, when he should be getting better. Jim when I first knew him, and he was then my closest friend (and, as on the New Yorker, my helper and benefactor) was, without listing attributes, just about the all-round nicest guy I've ever known. And then —what was it: blindness? drinking? something physical?—he got to the stage where Joe Sayre, in a piece for TIME could say, quoting someone maybe

invented, "he's the nicest guy in the world—till around nine o'clock in the evening."

And then, finally, well, outrage. And why?

With Ernest it seems to me it was a similar sort of thing, although, being a greater man and uncluttered with side issues, the thing seems simpler. As you know, he and I were fairly close friends back in the Paris days. I was one of those who "boxed with Hemingway." But we also walked about a good deal, visited back and forth (in Paris) and so on. But there was always something a little wary about him. As I see it now, and I believe I'm right, Ernest was one of those not-so-terribly-rare people who can't stand feeling obligated to anyone. If you did him a favor, you were dead, and it was on that note—when he turned so atrociously on Gertrude Stein (who had done so much for him) and on poor old Ford (same help and even worse treatment) that our friendship (as if that mattered) ended. He had also, with the first two novels, met success and had gotten out of the Quarter.

For some reason Coates did not save the letters he received from famous friends. He preferred not to trade on other people's names, and he may have felt—though here I have to guess—that the mere thought of preserving a correspondence for future readers would deprive it of frankness and spontaneity. Once a scholar asked to see his letters from Gertrude Stein. "Sorry, but I didn't keep them," Coates answered. "That's funny," the scholar said. "Miss Stein kept *your* letters." It was a merited rebuke, but a mild one, since the scholar realized that Coates had acted in accordance with his own strict notion of personal and literary ethics. Having resisted success, he continued to be the all-round nicest guy in the world, even after nine o'clock in the evening. He was deferent, unassuming, fond of playing immense but innocent jokes, and punctilious about returning favors. At other times, not often, he had lapses in kindness that were due, I think, to a compulsive need for going his own way. His friends often spoke of his sunny disposition, but his face in repose had a melancholy look and there must have been the streak of morbidity that was revealed in some of his best fiction, for instance, in *Wisteria Cottage* and in that often-anthologized tale, "The Fury."

I am still puzzled by these and other contradictions in his character and his writing. *Item,* to start a list of these, he was both solitary and gregarious. He loved boisterous parties and raffish companions, but I suspect that he was happiest when alone. *Item,* he was romantic by disposition, almost nypholeptic, dreaming for years of an impossibly beautiful woman in gray for whom he would eagerly sacrifice his future, but he was also a realist who worked, paid his debts, and had a hard observing eye for objects. *Item,* he was a city man who fled to the country, where he lived in tune with the earth and in

time with the seasons, as one learns from the lovely
first section of *Yesterday's Burdens;* but from time to
time he fled back to the city and roamed the streets from
Harlem to the Battery. And a final item chosen among
others: in spite of his boyhood travels over the country
and all those apprentice years in Paris, he remained in
some ways a Connecticut Yankee like his father. I think
of him as a craftsman, an inspired mechanic working
with words as his father had worked with pieces of
metal, choosing and calibrating, fitting together, then
grinding and polishing in the hope of achieving some
ultimate invention.

In his writing it is hard to distinguish the influence of
any single author (unless it might be James Thurber in
matter of style). He acknowledged a debt to Gertrude
Stein, but I cannot find in his work a single phrase that
he owed to her; perhaps what he had in mind was her
freedom of judgment. He owed another debt to the
Dadaists, among them Louis Aragon and his *Paysan de
Paris:* in Aragon's fashion he tried to be a wandering
peasant in Manhattan. Some of his work resembles the
early fiction of Kenneth Burke, but I think he arrived
independently at the same sort of devices. His impulse
was to invent, to do surprising things, to be accuratistic
and conversational while abandoning the pretense that
he was writing anything but fiction; then to give everything a consistent finish as if he were polishing steel.
Each work he produced was die-stamped with his own
trademark.

Among Coates's twelve books, *Yesterday's Burdens* has always been my favorite. It contains more of himself than the others: more of his contradictions, more of his inventiveness, more of his nympholepsy, more of his double feeling for city streets and the deep country. It is also a completed act rather than a mere novel. In the end it impresses me as a sort of leavetaking, almost a symbolic suicide.

One should read again a passage beginning on page 41 in which the author sets forth his program. "But let me tell you about this book I'm trying to write," he says, "in between bouts of book-reviewing":

> It's a novel, or rather a novel about a novel, or perhaps one might better describe it as a long essay discussing a novel that I might possibly write, with fragments of the narrative inserted here and there, by way of illustration or example.
>
> Or—again one might say—the attempt is to make it as nearly as possible a true example of the roman vécu. Nothing in it that I myself have not seen, heard, felt—or seen or felt in some other so vividly as almost to make the experience my own.
>
> The plot, of course, is the difficulty. You know my idea about plots—pick a good lively one and then forget about it. In this case, though, I don't think that formula would work. I have this young man, Henderson, and the process would seem to be to take him to the city and there lose him, as

thoroughly as possible. Or at least to reverse the usual method, and instead of trying to individualize him and pin him down to a story, to generalize more and more about him—to let him become like the figures in a crowd, and the crowd dispersing.

But isn't that, after all, the authentic thing—the thing that happens to all of us nowadays, and to all our friends?

"This book I'm trying to write" is *Yesterday's Burdens* —of course, of course—and its author is like a conjurer laying his cards face up on the table. He has every right to be confident that there are enough tricks up his sleeve to keep the audience amazed. One trick among others is this: Henderson is so thoroughly lost in the city that his story can be given three possible endings. He will be 1) reconciled with his wife, who has come back from Paris unseduced and without a divorce—or 2) shot and killed by his lover's husband—or 3) left alone despondent—jobless, probably—and will jump to his death from a high window. Coates inclines toward the third ending, but without making up his mind. "I never saw him again," he repeats on the last page, as if throwing up his hands.

Meanwhile the conjurer is palming another card, or item of information. He does not tell the reader, but does allow him to guess, that "this young man, Henderson"—at least in one of his aspects—is the author himself. In another aspect, the social one, Henderson is vaguely connected with James Thurber (or so Coates told his wife many years later). The connection with Coates himself is better documented in the story. Henderson is given Coates's birthday, April 6, his red hair, some of what we recognize from other books as his boyhood memories, and also, clearly, the group of his Village friends. He impresses us as being one side of Coates's past, and also what Coates might have become if he had chosen to stay in New York and earn a big income instead of escaping to a country house without running water. That is why one thinks of the book as a symbolic or vicarious suicide. In making Henderson a scapegoat burdened with the author's sins (or what he had come to regard as sins)—in letting him vanish into the crowd (and the crowd dispersing)—Coates is abolishing part of himself while hoping, one strongly feels, to be reborn into a different future.*

He thought that *Yesterday's Burden* was an ideal title for such a work, though his publisher didn't agree. His publisher was the Macaulay Company, a small house that specialized in mildly salacious novels and ghosted

---

*Death-and-rebirth was the underlying theme of many books published during the early depression years. Two of these were written by Coates's friends: *Towards a Better Life,* an extraordinary "novel in the form of declamations," by Kenneth Burke (1932), and my own *Exile's Return* (1934). One might also mention Waldo Frank's big turgid novel *The Death and Birth of David Markand* (1934).

267

autobiographies. Lee Furman, the head of the house—
we called him "Mr. Macaulay"—had been persuaded by
Coates's friend Matthew Josephson to add a few avant-
garde authors to his list. He thought they would lend it
distinction, and also he had a wistful idea that he could
sell their books if they were attractively priced and
labeled. Mr. Macaulay believed in the magic of titles.
"Let's have a big novel written to order," he told an
editorial meeting, "and let's give it a tremendous title—
you know, something that will make people think of *The
Good Earth* or *All Quiet on the Western Front*. Any
bright ideas?" Of course someone suggested "The Bad
Earth." "Or," Isidor Schneider said—he was the poet
who served as advertising manager—"what about 'All
Noisy on the Eastern Behind'?"

Mr. Macaulay was distressed by Coates's title. "This
year," he told the author—it was in 1933—"nobody wants
to hear about yesterday's burdens or any other burdens.
Can't you find something upbeat and catchy?" Coates
stammered a little, as always, but insisted on his down-
beat title, and Mr. Macaulay accepted it, though with
misgivings that he must have passed on to his salesmen.
He was an amiable businessman on the edge of failure,
and he hated arguments. Perhaps he was right about the
mood of the time, or perhaps he made himself right by
giving the book no advance promotion. It did receive
some appreciative reviews, including one I wrote for
The New Republic, but, on the whole, it attracted little

notice in a year when critics were arguing about proletarian literature. Like *Miss Lonelyhearts,* also published in 1933—and also dismissed as being "of the 1920s," a period then held in low esteem—it became an example of the good book that some people talked about, but almost nobody bought. It is my impression that most of the first and only printing was sold cheaply as overstock. Two years later the Macaulay Company went out of business—not because of *Yesterday's Burdens*—and the book was quietly interred. My tardily written review might have been the tribute spoken over a grave.

I had praised the book, but not nearly enough—so it seems to me now—and chiefly for the feeling it conveyed of a given social caste in a given year. The caste was the one to which Henderson belonged, the new caste composed of bright young people who had flocked to Manhattan and prospered there. "As American business entered the boom era," I wrote, "it needed more and more propagandists to help in the increasingly difficult task of selling more commodities each year to families that were given no higher wages to buy them with, and therefore had to be tempted with all the devices of art, literature, and science into bartering their future earnings for an automobile or a bedroom suite. Business needed public-relations counselors, it needed advertising artists and copywriters, it needed romancers to fill the pages of magazines in which its products were advertised, and illustrators to make the romance visible (and psychologists to explain how the whole process could be intensified); it needed stylists, designers, editors"; and I went on to say that in the boom years it conferred high rewards on not a few of these. There was a time when the bright young people, as a caste, regarded New York as a grand yearlong party given strictly for themselves. But their mood, as I observed and shared it, was changing even before the Crash, and many or most of them had come to be painfully dissatisfied with their lives.

The Crash is not mentioned in Coates's novel, though perhaps it can be sensed there as an undertone. As for the "given year" depicted, it is obviously not the year before the novel was published, considering that the narrator goes rambling through Manhattan without seeing breadlines or boarded-up stores. Coates was a slow writer who liked to mull over his impressions before setting them down, and the time of his story could only be 1930, the strange year that followed the Crash and served as an epilogue to the Boom. Hardly anything had changed on the surface of Henderson's world. Jobs could still be found in New York (or at least held on to); there were as many parties as ever (though more often with glum or violent sequels in the early-morning hours); and meanwhile everything was imperceptibly going to pieces, including long-established marriages and friendships.

"Often it seems I have no friends" is one of the "topic sentences" that Coates repeats with variations as if they were musical themes. At one point he continues:

—or rather, I have friends, but all of them have Watkins, Algonquin or Stuyvesant telephone numbers and live in the Village. Tonight, I will have none of them; I know so well what they are doing. I know so well those green-tinted apartments, the furniture that has so much the air of being fresh from the furniture store, the standing lamps arranged to illuminate the pages of the books no one ever has time to read in the easy chairs.

There will be greetings and ringings of the telephone, cocktails will be poured and drunk, cigarettes held in nervous fingers. Towards eight o'clock or later, women will be crowding before the mirror in the bathroom, men will be hunting out overcoats from the tangle of clothes on the bed in the alcove and shoving their arms into the sleeves; people will be going trailing laughter down the stairs. We shall all gather on the sidewalk in a little noisy cluster, deep down among the silent unfriendly houses.

It is a pleasure to transcribe those lines that suggest a vanished way of life. Each word is in the right place—as always in Coates's prose—and each phrase is an incantation against the danger of remaining in Henderson's world. It was in 1930 that Coates took flight into the Connecticut countryside, into a farming community already invaded by others whom Henderson might have

271

known. Few of the others made the same effort to put down new roots. Coates says of the invasion in another passage that conveys the feeling of the year, this time in country terms:

> On all sides one sees writers, painters, fashion designers buying acres of tillable land or pasture and dedicating them to the cultivation of sumac, goldenrod and blackberry brambles. Is it for revenge? The artist's tendencies, it would seem, are always atavistic: he would raze cities, he would remake New England into a wilderness. But what of the land itself?
>
> I sometimes feel a strange uneasiness: the trees look hostile, the very grass seems to regard me with a venomous air. I have bought these fields and doomed them to sterility. Can you tell me if there is anything in common law concerning the rights of the soil to expect careful husbandry on the part of its owner?

Those lines were written about an early stage of the invasion; sumac and goldenrod have now given way to second-growth forest. The New England countryside has changed as definitely as New York City, and much of it —between the new housing developments—has indeed become a wilderness crisscrossed by stone fences. Not a few books of the 1970s deal with efforts to reclaim portions of that wilderness for grazing or tillage, and they are echoes, as it were, of Coates's feeling about the soil.

In that respect and others—notably in the cards-on-the-table attitude revealed toward the art of fiction—*Yesterday's Burdens* has a prophetic quality, and this helps to explain why I admire it more today than when I reviewed it forty years ago. I had praised it then as a sort of contemporary history, as a subjective but accurate picture of a social order just on the point of being destroyed, or self-destroyed. Now it seems to me that the special point in time has been so well depicted, in a novel so full of inventions and yet so solidly put together, that the moment itself might have been cast in metal. And it seems to me too that *Yesterday's Burdens* is part of our heritage, not one of the major classics, but still a lasting book and, in its quiet way, essential.

Textual Note: The text of *Yesterday's Burdens* published here is a photo-offset reprint of the first printing (New York: Macaulay, 1933). No emendations have been made in the text.

M. J. B.